GIANTS OF THE SUN

Edited by Polly Nolan

MACMILLAN CHILDREN'S BOOKS

First published 2002 by Macmillan Children's Books
A division of Macmillan Publishers Limited
20 New Wharf Road, London N1 9RR
Basingstoke and Oxford
www.panmacmillan.com

Associated companies throughout the world

ISBN 0 330 39617 X

3 5 7 9 8 6 4 2

A CIP catalogue record for this book is available from the British Library.

Typeset by SX Composing DTP, Rayleigh, Essex
Printed and bound in Great Britain by Mackays of Chatham plc, Kent

For my brothers and sisters
Thanks . . . I think
PN

CONTENTS

RAINY PEOPLE

Marilyn Taylor

Jimmy Byrne was watching out for the glimmer man.

Perched on the window sill in the upstairs bedroom, he gazed down at the row of small brick houses fronting Stamer Street. Further down, on the bumpy cobbles, the regular football game was in progress with coats bundled up as makeshift goalposts.

Jimmy sighed as cheerful shouts echoed up into the chilly room. Why was it always himself and not Eamon, two years older, who was given this boring job of watching out for the glimmer man?

Jimmy had never actually seen the alarming, uniformed figure from the gas company on his tell-tale orange bicycle; but Jimmy knew that if he spotted him, he was to yell a warning to his nana and to all the neighbours, so that they could turn off the gas before the glimmer man knocked.

Jimmy's da said that rationing gas was pointless because, like Nana, half of Dublin was busily cooking during the 'off' times, using the tiny drop of gas left in the pipes, even though it was switched off at the mains. The 'glimmer' they called it – a weak little blue flame on which, downstairs at that moment, a tin of beans was slowly heating for the tea.

If you were caught using the 'glimmer', his nana said, the gas company would cut off your gas altogether and then you couldn't cook anything at all. 'And how,' she demanded, 'would I feed a hungry man and two growing boys?'

Jimmy knew that this and other puzzling and scary changes in their lives were all down to the Emergency. That's what it was called here, though everywhere else, as Jimmy's teacher had explained, it was called the War.

It was not just the glimmer man. There were the newly-built concrete bomb shelters in the streets; the gas masks that were supposed to protect you but made people look like monsters. And the shortages: tea, fuel, paper, chocolate, cigarettes; his da would walk miles to the shop where he could get his pack of five Woodbines.

Because there was no petrol, people had to use horse-drawn carts and two-wheel cabs, or bikes, or even donkey carts. Coal was in short supply; in Phoenix Park, huge heaps of turf had appeared overnight, for home fires.

Across the Irish Sea, Britain was locked in a desperate fight – the War – against Nazi

Germany, which wanted to take over and terrorize Europe and the world. Here in Ireland, we were staying out of the War, so we just called it the Emergency. But whatever it was called, his da said it meant that the dreaded Nazi troops might invade Ireland – like they had so many other countries – and Jimmy knew this was something to be feared.

Jimmy's friend Seán and the others thought the Emergency was exciting, like an adventure story out of the *Beano* or *Dandy* comics.

But for Jimmy the Emergency wasn't an exciting adventure. Nothing was, any more. Not since the dreadful time last winter, when his mammy had coughed and coughed, growing thinner and paler from the TB, until the only things he could still recognize were her sad smile and gentle voice.

When she was sent to the Sanatorium to get better, Jimmy had missed her dreadfully; missed her gently washing his scabby knees in the metal bath or ruffling his hair as he did his homework at the kitchen table.

Da and Nana had said that she would be sent home from the Sanatorium as soon as she was better. But, instead, one day Nana had told him his mammy had gone on to a better place, where she would never be sick again, and from where she would watch over them all.

After Mammy died, Jimmy asked himself how he could ever trust them again – Da and Nana. He felt lost and lonely and fearful of what might happen next. And sometimes, after a night of dark, unhappy dreams – often about his mammy – he found that something really bad had happened: without knowing it, he had wet the bed.

Each morning, as soon as he awoke to the smell of frying bacon wafting up from the kitchen and the bang of the front door as his da left for work at the Ever Ready battery factory, a feeling of fear clutched at Jimmy's stomach.

On the bad mornings, when he woke lying in a warm, damp patch, he sometimes wished he could follow his mammy to Heaven, where maybe this jumble of troubles would magically disappear.

'Jimmy, come down!'

Roused from his thoughts by Nana's shout, he slid thankfully off the window sill. His watch was over, the glimmer man hadn't come and the tea was ready.

Jimmy cheered up as he and Eamon tucked into baked beans and thick slices of coarse, dark bread which, his nana grumbled, was all you could get now there was no white flour. But at least there was home-made apple jelly from windfall apples that he, Seán and Eamon had collected in the gardens of the big houses down by the canal.

Afterwards, they listened to *Question Time* on the wireless, not that they knew any of the answers. But the record programme which followed – with John McCormack, whom Nana, listening with tears in her eyes, insisted had the voice of an angel – was the signal for Jimmy and Eamon to escape from the cramped kitchen. They hurried to join the games of Cowboys and Indians or of hurling, which took place in their street on the long summer evenings.

The next morning – a Saturday – there was no wet patch when Jimmy woke. His heart lightened and, jumping out of bed on to the cold lino, he gabbled his prayers and made a dash for the toilet out in the back yard.

'Wash your hands,' said Nana in her old flannel dressing-gown, her grey hair escaping from its bun, as she hurried to cook eggs and bacon rashers for them all before the gas went off again.

Da sat at the kitchen table, last night's *Evening Mail* propped in front of him. As

Eamon and Jimmy shovelled in their food, Da looked up from the racing news and said gruffly to Jimmy, 'Well, young fella, you've a treat coming up!'

Jimmy looked up warily. Treats were rare in Stamer Street. Maybe he'd get a penny. He'd rush to the corner shop to buy a bright yellow lollipop or a string of liquorice.

Eamon was beginning to look like thunder. 'Why's he getting a treat?' he grumbled. 'I suppose it's because he's such a baby—'

'There's no call for that kind of talk,' snapped Nana.

'You're over the age,' Da told Eamon. 'The under-tens in the youth club are going camping for a week in Shankill.'

'Shankill?' said Jimmy hesitantly. 'Where's that?'

'It's the seaside,' said Nana, smiling. 'You'll go on the train and sleep in a tent. It's for kiddies that never had a holiday.'

Jimmy felt anxious. 'Who'll be in charge?' Silently he added, *and what'll happen if I wet the bed?*

'There'll be grown-ups, helpers,' said his da. 'The camp leader will be Mr Brown, he knows all about tents and suchlike.' He lowered his voice. 'And sure everything's better in the fresh air, even . . .' He stopped.

But Jimmy knew he meant, '. . . even the bed-wetting.'

'And remember,' whispered Nana to Jimmy. 'Your mammy will be watching over you.' She brushed her eyes with her hand. 'She used to love the sea.'

A week later, Jimmy, excited but nervous, was waiting at Harcourt Street Station for the Bray train, along with Seán and twenty other boys and girls yelling, giggling, pushing and shoving.

This was definitely better than school, he thought, or watching for the glimmer man. Nana had carefully packed his clothes, with spare underwear (in case of accidents, she whispered), a tin plate and mug, jam sandwiches and an apple.

Eamon had muttered, 'Watch out for cows, they could be bulls.' Then, as a peace offering, he had thrust two small squares of a melting Cadbury's penny chocolate bar into Jimmy's hand. But he couldn't resist adding, 'Bet it'll be really boring.'

At the station, Da patted Jimmy's shoulder. 'Have a good time, young fella.' He held out a rough, work-worn hand in which lay a shining silver sixpence. 'And don't be worrying.'

Sitting in the steam train beside Seán,

Jimmy clutched his sixpence and tried to ignore the familiar sick feeling. From her seat opposite, Annie Walsh, one of the helpers, who knew his nana, smiled over at him reassuringly. Then the leader, Mr Brown, a tall, heavy man with white hair and horn-rimmed glasses, and an older boy, Frank O'Kelly, started a singsong. Joined by some of the other passengers, they all roared out the chorus of 'Danny Boy'.

Outside the train window, the houses and streets jerked past, gradually making way for trees and green meadows and corn fields, all new sights for Jimmy and most of the others.

At Shankill station, laden with rucksacks and bundles, they climbed down. Standing on the platform, they gazed around them at the flowery fields in a wondering silence, broken only by birdsong and the faint hum of bees in the hedgerow.

Hoisting his rucksack on to his back and anxiously keeping a lookout for cows, Jimmy followed Seán in the line of boys and girls trudging up the hillside to the muddy field that was to be their campsite.

Flinging down their burdens, they rushed across to the bushes of creamy hawthorn at the far end of the field. And there, far below them, Jimmy caught his first and never to be forgotten sight of the sea – a wide rippling expanse streaked with blue and green, fading in the distance into the softer blue of the sky.

On that first day, there was so much to be done that Jimmy hardly had time to think. The older boys helped the grown-ups to put up the canvas tents. Then with wooden mallets they all banged in the pegs that held the tents down.

'Jimmy, you and Seán and a couple of girls come with me to the farmhouse,' called Frank O'Kelly. On the way back, laden with fresh eggs and milk brought from the farmer's wife, they picked their way through the squishy cowpats, passing close to some of the cows. One of them stared at Jimmy in a bored way, and then bent its head, tore up a mouthful of grass and began to munch. The girl in front of him, her dark glossy hair in ringlets tied back with a pink bow, gave a little whimper.

'They won't harm you unless you mess with them,' said Frank firmly. 'Isn't that right, lads?'

'Sure,' said Seán. 'Nothing to be afraid of.'

Jimmy nodded agreement and, summoning up all his courage, said softly to her, 'What's your name, then?'

'Peggy.' And she gave him a shy grin.

When they got back to the camp, the others were out collecting dead wood for the camp fire. The grown-ups had dug the latrines – smelly pits with wooden planks across them – which served as toilets. Peggy, walking beside Jimmy, wrinkled her nose as they passed them.

A sudden memory shot into Jimmy's mind of the warm, wet patch in his bed at home some mornings. If an 'accident' happened here, maybe everyone would hear about it, and jeer at him, maybe even Peggy. His carefree mood darkened as he plodded back to the dining tent where sausages were being fried with bread for their supper.

All through the meal and the cheerful noisy singsong that followed, anxiety about the night ahead filled his mind. Even when Peggy waved at him across the camp fire, and Seán gave him a grin and a nudge, Jimmy sat silent.

At bedtime, with lagging steps, he joined the crowd surging towards the tents.

A voice said, 'Jimmy Byrne, you're over there in Tent B.' Annie Walsh, looking young and boyish in check shirt and khaki shorts, led him to it. Jimmy bent down and crawled inside, to find Frank and four nervous-looking young boys.

Then Frank said, 'Now, lads, this tent is for the rainy people.' They all stared at him. He grinned. 'It's for anyone that might have a bit of an accident in the night. You're not to worry, because the sleeping bags have all got waterproof liners.' No one said a word.

Frank went on, 'I just want you to know, I was one of the rainy ones myself when I was your age.' They stared at him.

Jimmy heard himself say, 'You mean . . . ?'

Frank laughed. 'Yeah, we all grow out of it in the end.' Grins appeared on some of the faces. Jimmy felt a rush of relief. Frank went on, 'The trick is not to worry about it. If you don't worry, it hardly ever happens.'

Cosy in his sleeping bag, Jimmy slept deeply, and dreamed of his mammy, up in heaven, looking down at the dark tents of the camp, under the stars.

The days at the camp were so filled with work and fun that Jimmy wished they would never end. There were games, walks and competitions organized by Annie, Frank and the other helpers. And each day ended with songs and jokes and stories around the camp fire.

One day they went on a long hike to the beach.

'Only two days till we go home,' said

Seán, as they picked their way across the sharp stones to paddle in the icy water among the strings of slimy seaweed.

'Wish it was longer,' muttered Jimmy, offering round the sticky wine gums he had bought with his sixpence. He had made friends with the other boys from his tent, and with Peggy, who had now attached herself to Jimmy and Seán, following them around adoringly.

Best of all, Jimmy had had only one 'accident', which had been passed off by Frank as being of no account. Maybe Frank was right, thought Jimmy, as he laced up his boots for the hike back to the camp; the trick was not to worry.

Sometimes he heard Mr Brown and the other grown-ups talking in low voices about bombing raids and a Nazi invasion. But here among the golden gorse bushes, close to the sea – grey today, with frothy white caps on the waves – Jimmy hardly ever thought of any of that. Even when he dreamed of his mammy, she no longer looked so sad.

The last day at camp was a Sports Day, with all sorts of races – wheelbarrow, egg-and-spoon, relays and long jump.

'There'll be a surprise tonight after the singsong,' said Annie, as they sat later in the kitchen tent, peeling potatoes for supper.

Though they begged her to say what it was, she would only repeat, 'Wait till after dark.'

That night the sky was like a dark canopy, the moon hidden behind scudding clouds. The camp fire had died down to glowing embers. All the grown-ups had gone across the field and were busy behind the hawthorn hedge.

Then there was a shout, and up into the sky whooshed a shower of sparklers, followed by a rocket, and then more rockets, bursting with loud echoing explosions into streams of blue, green and red, silver and gold, and fading into smoky trails. They all cheered, watching as more sparklers and rockets shot up, and then a spinning Catherine wheel, shining and glittering and glowing with colour against the velvety night sky.

Jimmy had never seen anything so beautiful. Maybe his mammy could see the firework display, he thought; she would be closer to it than they were, down here on the ground. Beside him, Peggy turned to him with shining eyes. 'Wasn't that brilliant, Jimmy?' she said, slipping her hand into his. It was a long time since Jimmy had felt so happy.

A few hours later, he was wakened from a deep sleep by shouts and the sound of something crashing through the hedge. Round him the others stirred. Frank leaped up and grabbed his torch. Hastily pulling a coat over his pyjamas, he dashed out of the tent.

Could it be the cows? Jimmy wondered.

Everyone was awake now, wriggling out of their sleeping bags. 'What's going on?' They hurried outside, to find pandemonium.

Surrounding the campsite were about twenty soldiers in green army uniforms and tin helmets, faces blackened, holding torches, and what looked like real rifles. At the gate to the field stood a menacing armoured car.

Two army officers, shoulder bars on their uniforms, were deep in conversation with Mr Brown, Frank and some of the grown-ups.

Seán appeared with Peggy in tow, her hair awry, a cardigan over her nightie. 'What's happening, Jimmy?' she whispered, on the verge of tears. 'Is it the Invasion?'

Jimmy put his arm round her. 'Don't worry,' he said, trying to push down his own fears, which were beginning to rise to the surface. Had the Nazis come? Was Ireland now going to be in the War, instead of just the Emergency? Were there going to be air raids? Were Nana and Da and Eamon all right?

Around them the deep dark of the night was criss-crossed with torchlight. In the eerie glow the soldiers stood watching. Bewildered campers milled about, murmuring in little groups.

Then, above the hubbub, came the booming voice of Mr Brown. There was immediate silence.

'Campers, there's nothing to be afraid of,' he said. 'These are Irish soldiers. There's been a bit of a mix-up.' He paused. 'Some people saw the fireworks and thought the Nazis had invaded.'

There was a ripple of relieved laughter. But Mr Brown and the officers looked serious. 'We thought we had permission for the fireworks. On behalf of all of us at the camp, I want to apologize for any trouble caused.'

In the burst of chatter that followed, Jimmy patted Peggy's shoulder, 'See, I told you not to worry.' It was something he couldn't imagine having said to anyone a week before. Then, he was always the one who was frightened. But since the camp, he realized he felt more confident about things, not so scared. And if the real Invasion came, he'd just face it along with everything else.

'Come on, Jimmy, let's ask those soldiers if we can look at their rifles,' said Seán. He grinned. 'Wait till they hear about this in Stamer Street.'

And followed by the faithful Peggy, they went over to where a group of soldiers was joking and chatting with the campers who crowded around them.

Just for a moment, Jimmy stopped and looked up at the night sky. The clouds had cleared, and he could see bright patterns of stars, which Frank had explained to them – the Great Plough, the Little Plough, and Orion with three stars at his belt.

Jimmy knew his mammy was up there and, somehow, he was sure she was looking down and smiling.

THE JEWEL BOX

Polly Devlin

When the Fenians came to burn the house down it was dark and it was cold, and Nancy was frightened. She didn't care about the house, though she loved it, nor was she worried about her parents. Her parents were, as all parents must be, very brave when standing up to the thugs who woke them in the night and ordered them out of their warm beds into the freezing dark. These men would give the family time to get out, but nothing would stop them torching the house and with it all its lovely, silky, grand contents, gathered over centuries of travel, of accumulation.

No; she was frightened for her little dog in case he barked and bit and annoyed the burners-down and they burned him too. Plug was fearless – a little, foxy, long-nosed scrap of a thing. He was always at Nancy's heels, usually as they roamed through the woods and across the fields looking for pheasants, hares and rabbits to accost and, as Plug hoped, to savage horribly, though he never got anywhere near close enough. He could give them a good run for their money anyhow. No matter how far he roamed,

Nancy had only to whisper his name for him to be at her feet within minutes. It was as though a thread quivered between them; the slightest twitch and Plug was there.

Nancy loved hearing about how Plug had been found, though the story also made her shiver. How her mother, driving towards Limerick, had seen a man come out at the back of a squalid encampment of caravans and lean over a water trough with something small, something moving, in his hand. She had leaped from the car. She had not been in time to save the first three tiny pups, but the last one was still struggling, trying to keep its little blind head above the surface. She had snatched it out and put the tiny, drenched morsel under her sweater and confronted the startled man furiously. But, for all her fury, her mother said to Nancy that it was the way of that world; too many puppies born each year to too many dogs who followed the caravans. Generally they were drowned in a bag tied at the top. Plug had been lucky.

'I'll take this,' Nancy's mother had said, glaring at the man and patting the shivering lump under her sweater, wet and still but drying out, she hoped, against her body heat, though dying out seemed the more likely judging from the desperate coldness of the thing against her skin.

'That's a valuable wee dog,' the man said, grinning wickedly.

Nancy's mother's mouth dropped open. 'You were,' she was almost speechless, 'you were flaming drowning it.'

'All the same there's Pomeranian in him. He'll be a nice, wee, handy dog,' he said.

And he was. A nice, handy, wee dog, never making a fuss, but always on his mark, always beside Nancy who was at the centre of his life. Plug had been saved from drowning. Now he must be saved from fire.

Nancy had always known that some day the Fenians would come and get them. Bridie, who had looked after her since she was born, had told her so. The Fenians were rebel Irishmen fighting a guerrilla war against the British government, which ruled all Ireland at that time. She often heard her father declaim against them. 'I'd hang the lot of them,' he'd bellow when he was poring over the *Irish Times* at breakfast, reading of another Anglo-Irish family frog-marched out of their homes; mourning the loss of another great house, burned to the ground the night before. These families were being forced to go to England, even though they had never lived there, and neither had their forebears, not for centuries.

'All the same,' Bridie said when Nancy spoke of the unfairness of it, 'All the same, they have the grand English names and their kin all lives over there, and don't they think of England as their mother country? So they can go back to it. They have somewhere to go back to, the lot of them; they left us nowhere to go but Hell or Connacht or Amerikay or Liverpool. So let them go back to England. *And good riddance,*' she added under her breath. But Nancy heard and her heart was torn between love of her Bridie who was Irish-Irish and her parents who were this strange thing, Anglo-Irish.

'I can't see the point of being hyphenated,' Nancy said one morning. 'Anglo-Irish. I mean, one should be either Irish or English, but not in-between.'

'We're not in-between,' her father had roared. 'We're both. You don't call the French-Martins either one thing or the other. They're of both the French family and the Martin family, and proud of each side. And that's how it's been for a thousand years.'

'Well, they should choose which,' Nancy said. She could have said – but didn't – that there wasn't one of the French-Martins who was not mealy-mouthed or wishy-washy, their big house topsy-turvy as though their very name made them live in a hyphenated world. *I'll always live in Ireland*, Nancy thought, *whatever happens, and be Irish and live in a caravan outside Limerick, if needs be, and rescue dogs out of water troughs*. She hugged Plug closer.

Now she stood in her dark bedroom, blinking, frightened, looking at the masked men in the fading firelight, and holding Plug by the nose to try to keep him from barking. Plug wriggled furiously, desperate to get down, to savage the men.

Her mother, in her dressing-gown, pushed past them. She rushed over to Nancy and held her. 'At least let me light my daughter's lamp,' she said. 'So she can see what she's doing.'

'You don't need to be lighting no lamps,' one of the men answered, without moving. 'You'll have plenty enough light in a minute or two. You'll be able to see twenty miles by the light we'll give you.' The other men laughed.

Her father appeared behind her mother in the doorway with another light. His small moustache seemed to be more bristly than ever, caught in its own shadow. His hands were tied behind his back. 'See here, you Fenian thugs,' he said, and his wife turned and hushed him.

Nancy stared at the men. So here they were, as Bridie had prophesied. But she hadn't described their appearance, their horrible handkerchiefs tied over their mouths, their hats jammed low over their foreheads, their menace. They came further into the room. Nancy saw they all carried guns.

One man said, 'Be out with you, Miss, and you'll come to no harm.' He put a hand on her shoulder. It was too much for Plug who, seeing him dare to touch the person he loved more than life itself, launched himself out of Nancy's arms and shot like a rocket towards his neck. The man, startled, jumped back and fell hard against the man behind him, knocking him over. His gun went off. The noise of the explosion beside her was excruciating. Nancy had never heard anything like it; she felt as though her ears had been ripped open. Nor had she ever felt anything like the pain she was now feeling in her arm which, she saw as she fell to the ground, was hanging at a crazy angle. Plug, who had been howling with rage and fear beside her, now began to whimper.

Nancy had fallen on top of the man lying on the floor. His hat and handkerchief had come off in the confusion, and she saw herself looking into the green, dark-lashed eyes of Tomás, the young man who worked in the stables. Nancy had been thinking of him a lot recently. A few weeks ago she had seen him taking off on Volcano, the big roan horse her father had lately bought and which no one could master. No one but Tomás. First time out, he and Volcano had soared over enormous fences effortlessly, flying across the fields. Nancy had been more impressed than she liked to admit. It was she who had ridden Volcano with just such style in her dreams.

But this, now, was the stuff of nightmares. 'I'm sorry, Miss,' Tomás whispered. 'It's nothing personal.' He pulled his handkerchief up again. No one else had seen his face. Nancy rolled on to the floor, the pain in her arm stabbing. Her mother kneeled beside her, talking, soothing, stroking. Her father was cursing with rage at the men, screaming at them to untie him to fetch a doctor.

Her mother said quietly, 'Please let my husband go. We need a doctor as soon as possible. And we must staunch the wound.' She began to tear the sheets off the bed to make a bandage. Nancy closed her eyes. She heard someone say, 'It's only a flesh wound. 'Tis only a graze. You can go for the doctor when we've left.'

Nancy opened her eyes and tried to turn her head to look at her arm. The acrid smell of gun smoke in the room was clearing, but even in the dim lights there seemed to be a lot of blood about. Her blood. She felt white and sick and thought she might faint. As her eyes closed she saw Bridie pushing past the men into the room. 'Sweet God,' she cried, 'you have the child killt. That's some way to fight for Ireland, to be shooting children.' She kneeled beside Nancy. 'Wait,' she said to one of the masked men. 'Wait till I tell your mother what you're doing for the Cause. Shooting wee girls. She'll have something to say to you.'

'We didn't shoot her,' one man stammered, shuffling from foot to foot. Nancy wondered if he was the man with the mother. 'It happened with the dog lepping and herself falling.'

'Give my head peace,' Bridie said. 'You'll be saying it was her fault next. Let us get the child out of the house and let the master go and get the doctor.'

'For the love of God,' another man said. 'Will you all hurry up before the police are upon us, never mind the doctor. You could have heard that blast all over the country.'

The men stood to one side as Tomás, in his mask, and old Bridie carried Nancy out to the lawn, her mother behind them, and laid her down under the big cedar tree. She saw her father being led out. The men had gagged him. For the first time Nancy began to cry. Tomás kneeled beside her.

'Don't you be fretting,' he said to her gently. 'No harm will come to him. We have to gag him for his own good, jumping about like a bantam cockerel. Phelim there has a bad temper if he's annoyed and your father was annoying him, telling him he had no right to be here.'

'Wouldn't you be annoyed,' Nancy said, 'if someone came in the middle of the night to burn your house and frighten your dog? And then if that someone shot you?' she added almost as an afterthought, looking at the strip of sheet tied in a bandage below her elbow.

'I would, Miss,' he said, 'and we are annoyed. And that's what this is all about. We've been annoyed for hundreds of years. Can you not understand? What we're doing to you now, you and your kind did to us over and over again. Only you did it to the whole country. We were the ones who lived here, this was our land, Ireland, and you took it and scorched it and made it to be English and gave us nothing – only hard words and dry bread and bad punishment. We starved to death in our own rich country, and you living on the fat of the land. And now we've come to take it back.' He put out his hand to touch her shoulder, but Plug bared his teeth. 'All the same,' Tomás said gently, 'that's a handy wee dog you have there.'

'We got him out of a trough in Limerick,' Nancy said. She was feeling very weak.

'Did you indeed,' he said admiringly. 'He's a right wee talisman.'

'Stop parleying with the enemy,' her father roared at Nancy. He'd struggled until the gag had worked free. 'If I had my way, I'd shoot the lot of you. What right have you to come to my house and threaten us? By God, I'll have you strung up if it's the last thing I do.'

Nancy glanced at Tomás. He said, serious, 'It will be the last thing he says if he goes on taunting Phelim. Phelim has a very short temper.' Nancy looked to where Tomás was looking. Phelim was a big man. A big, angry man with a gun.

'We have more right to come here nor you have to be here,' Phelim said, putting his face close to her father's. 'This place was mine and my forebears' before you stole it from us. You're lucky we don't shoot the lot of you, like you shot us. Shot us and starved us like dogs when you took our land.'

'You hooligan,' Nancy's father spluttered. 'How dare you – we've lived in this house for three hundred years.'

'You still stole it,' Phelim said. 'It doesn't matter how long you've had a thing, if it was stole in the first place, it will be stole in the second and the third, down to where you are now, kicking under the stars. Go back to where you came from and leave Ireland to the Irish and no harm will come to you.'

'I'd rather die in Ireland than live in England,' her father said.

There was a silence. Phelim looked at him with something like respect. He untied him. 'Go you now and get a doctor for your daughter,' he said, 'but you must walk it. And if we hear you come back with the police, we will shoot her.'

Her father set off down the drive at a fast run, not looking back. Nancy and her mother watched the masked men go back into the house. She saw them go from room to room, their silhouettes against windows. Presently, flames began to appear in the bottom rooms of the great house, flickers first and then strong, hot flames. Nancy had not realized what a noise a fire could make – overwhelming, roaring, like being trapped in a tunnel with a train going through. Her

31

arm was hurting terribly. Plug was whimpering again. She wanted to whimper too, but she bit her lip. 'Soldier's daughter,' she said to herself, as she had heard her father say to her so often whenever she was doing something difficult; and then the rallying cry of his regiment, to get their courage up, 'Steady the Buffs'. She whispered the magic words under her breath.

The men came running round from the back of the house. 'Move back,' one shouted, waving his arms. 'Move, move, before the roof comes down on the top of you.'

Bridie and her mother lifted Nancy as gently as they could, back and away from the house. Through a haze of smoke and pain she watched the house burn and with it the treasures and trivia in those long, beautiful rooms that opened on to the river. The lovely paintings of stallions and landscapes and ancestors; the long, scalloped-leather lines of books; the faded, looped, silk brocade curtains; the plasterwork ceilings; the intricately patterned carpets brought back from India; the enormous, sinister umbrella-stand which had once been an elephant's foot; the four-poster bed with its ostrich plumes and crowns made for Queen

Victoria's visit – the accumulations of three hundred years. Three centuries of life that her ancestors had lived, yet they were still strangers and interlopers. Three centuries going up in smoke and all she could do was watch. Plug sat close beside her, licking at her hand. Her Irish talisman.

Tomás, unrecognizable to her mother in his mask and hat, came urgently out of the flames and the darkness carrying a big, leather box. He set it down on the grass beside her mother.

'I rescued this for you,' he said gently. 'It's all I could save, but it is precious to you and yours.' He looked towards Nancy and smiled, his green eyes full of something other than hate and revenge.

Nancy blushed. *I hate him*, she thought, *Fenian thug; he is my enemy*. But the words had no meaning. She sounded just like her father, and where had that got him?

And then Tomás was gone, racing towards the gate through which the others had disappeared. There was the sound of a lorry revving up and leaving.

Nancy lay deeper in the grass; she prayed the doctor would come quickly. Her mother was making an odd noise beside her. Was she laughing or crying? Nancy looked at her. She was doing both at the same time, shaking her head, sniffing, wiping her eyes. Nancy made an effort to speak, to try to cheer her up. 'At least he saved something; you have your jewel box.'

'Oh yes. He rescued my jewel box.' Her mother made that strange sound again, half despair, half humour. 'You tell her, Bridie.'

'Sure he wasn't to know,' Bridie said and then went silent.

'He didn't rescue the jewels,' her mother said. She brought the box over beside Nancy and opened it. They looked into a jumble of brown envelopes and invoices. 'I kept them the wrong way round, you see, for safekeeping . . . to try to fool burglars. Ironic to think of it. My jewels were in a box marked Bills. And the bills, the record of every penny we owe, well, I stuffed them into the jewel box. My own silly fault.'

Nancy and her mother both stared at the leather box with its cargo of debts and then at the house leaping in on itself, folding down into its own devastating sparkle, the flaming sky above it, the whole countryside illuminated by the bonfire of burning history. Behind them they heard the doctor's car coming up the drive.

FOLLY

Maeve Friel

. . . suddenly a train was bearing down upon them, headlamps full on. Liam, Thomas and Marcus pressed themselves hard against the greasy black wall, their mouths open in a silent scream.

Thomas and Liam had been friends since first class. Thomas lived with his mother, a history teacher. His father had left home the year before and lived in a flat in the city centre with a wide-screen television. Thomas spent every other weekend with him, sometimes watching videos, but most often visiting museums or old jails, places that his father had read about in the Sunday newspaper supplements. He kept clippings about them pinned to a cork noticeboard in his kitchen. When Thomas was older, he was going to write a book called Things Boys Do *Not* Want To Do on Saturdays.

For the first few months after his parents separated, Thomas hoped that they would get back together again, but recently, looking through the open door of his mother's bedroom, he had seen that the two pillows on her bed were now on top of each other instead of side by side. He wasn't coming back.

Liam lived a few doors away. His father worked in a smart pub called The Big Bad Wolf. At breakfast he had been telling Liam about a famous model who had been in the night before. He was always on about his celebrity customers, Man U footballers, pop stars, visiting Hollywood actors. Sometimes he even brought home autographs scribbled on beer mats or the backs of bar bills that Liam was able to sell or trade at school. That morning his mother had been very snappy. She was pregnant with twins, so she was huge and fed up because she never got out and Liam's father was never at home.

'I don't want to hear another thing about supermodels or how many bottles of champagne they ordered. All I want is for these twins to get a move on,' she said, snatching his dad's cup of coffee out of his hand and pouring it down the sink.

Liam said he was going to the park with Thomas.

Marcus had recently moved to the city – his parents were Irish, but they had lived in England for years. Out of the blue they had announced they were moving to Dublin.

'There are fantastic opportunities there now,' they said. 'You'll love it, Marcus.' But Marcus was far from happy with his new life. He missed his friends. At school he was teased about his accent. Posh Boy, they called him. And, as if that wasn't bad enough, he had to learn Irish, which sounded absolutely mad.

His dad smiled when Marcus told him he hated Dublin and everything about it. 'Don't worry, son. We'll make an Irishman of you yet,' he said. 'You'll love it here when you settle in.'

I'm not going to love it here, Marcus thought to himself. *And I'm never going to settle in*. But he didn't say it out loud.

That Saturday morning, he was lying on the grass in the park watching a wispy trail of jet exhaust melting slowly in the sky overhead and thinking that it would only take an hour to get to London, when two boys from his class suddenly loomed over him.

'Oh, hello there, Posh Boy,' Thomas said, twisting his mouth and speaking in a ridiculous sort of Prince Charles accent. 'Fancy meeting you here!'

'Get lost,' said Marcus.

'He's only messing,' said Liam, thrusting

an open bag of smoky bacon crisps in Marcus's face. 'Do you want one?'

They threw themselves down on the grass, one on either side of him. Marcus froze, thinking they were planning to jump him and duff him up. He casually raised himself on to his elbows and considered making a run for it. Beside him, Liam rolled over on to his stomach and began to poke at the corners of his crisp bag with a wet finger. Thomas was sending text messages, his thumb stabbing rapidly at the buttons of his mobile.

What are they up to? Marcus wondered uneasily. *Are even more of them going to turn up?*

But nothing happened. They just lay there and watched the massive hulk of the superferry approaching Dun Laoghaire harbour. DART trains passed every few minutes, whistling as they came into the station. A seagull crash-landed on the roof of the bandstand with a half-eaten hamburger clenched in its claws and, immediately, more gulls arrived flapping and screaming, pecking and biting one another as they tried to snatch the bun. The din was terrible.

After a while, there seemed to be an unspoken agreement that it was time to leave. Thomas put his phone away. Liam scrunched his crisp bag into a ball and tossed it over his shoulder.

'Are you coming?' he said to Marcus, jerking his head towards the sea. Marcus nodded. They walked down to the bottom of the park, strolled past the DART station and crossed the pedestrian stone bridge to the seaward side of the tracks.

There was no beach, just rocks covered in slippery seaweed, encrusted with tiny, black mussel shells. They squelched their way across them in single file, holding their arms out like tightrope walkers to keep their balance. The seaweed sacs popped beneath their trainers like bubble-wrap bursting.

A few hundred metres on, Marcus stopped and pointed at an odd little building at the top of the cliff above them. 'What's that?' he asked. 'That thing that looks like a Greek temple.'

Liam shrugged. 'It's a wrecked church, I think.'

'No, it isn't,' said Thomas. 'It's called a folly. Mum said it belonged to some lord who used to own all the land round here ages ago. He made the government build it for him when they took his land to build the first railway.'

'How do you get up to it?'

'There used to be a bridge over the tracks from the other side, but it's not there any more. Anyway, you can't go near it. It's not allowed.'

Marcus raised an eyebrow. 'Says who?' he said.

They walked around the foot of the cliff, looking for some way up. Just as they were on the point of giving up, they came across an old, broken jetty and, beside it, the crumbling remains of stone steps that must once have gone all the way up to the top of the cliff. There was a rusting barbed-wire fence with a lopsided notice hanging on it. 'Danger', the notice declared, 'Keep Out'. The lettering was nearly illegible from years of being battered by salt wind and rain.

Thomas kicked down the bottom line of barbed wire and held up the top one to make a big enough gap to clamber through. 'Right,' he said, grinning from ear to ear and doing his Prince Charles impression again. 'Anyone for a spot of mountaineering?'

It was a hard climb, especially where whole sections of the steps had fallen away. Sometimes they had to crawl on all fours, groping for something solid to hold on to, kicking at the ground to make toeholds, hauling each other over the difficult bits and all the time getting scratched by brambles.

They arrived at the top, panting, exhausted and exhilarated.

Close up, the folly was in bits. Its pillars were crumbling and the roof had fallen in in places. The walls were covered with graffiti and spray-painted with swirling day-glo signatures. At first they thought there was no way to get inside, for the front door had been bricked up, but round the back there was a high window with all the panes knocked out.

Thomas dragged himself up on to the window sill by his fingertips and helped pull the other two up beside him. With all three of them pushing and pulling and kicking, it was easy to break the wooden window frame and jump down. Inside, the floor was littered with broken glass, beer cans, cider bottles and piles of dirty-grey ashes.

'Ugh,' said Liam, holding his nose. 'It stinks of cat's pee.'

'I don't think it's a cat,' said Thomas. He pointed to a pile of blankets in a corner. 'I think there's somebody living here.'

'No way,' said Liam. 'Nobody could live in a dump like this.'

'Hey, you guys, look at this.' Marcus, who had been rummaging around in another corner, dragged a battered old nylon suitcase into the middle of the room. 'What do you think is inside it?'

'Treasure?' said Thomas sarcastically. 'Or maybe the long-lost Irish Crown Jewels?'

'Shut up,' said Marcus, fiddling with the lock on the zip fastener. 'I just want to see, that's all.'

'Well then, give it here,' said Thomas. He picked up a piece of jagged glass from the floor and slashed the bag from one end to the other.

Liam and Marcus glanced uneasily at each other, then at Thomas, then at the bag. And suddenly they were seized by a sort of madness. They fell on the bag, pulling out its contents and flinging them right, left and centre. There was no treasure, just some old shirts and sweaters, a few books, a pair of shoes, a razor and a small mirror, an open packet of cream crackers and a half-empty bottle of some clear liquid.

'That's vodka,' said Liam, sniffing.

'You know what I think?' said Marcus. 'Thomas must be right. There is someone squatting here. We'd better get going.'

They were rounding the corner of the folly, heading for the steps to begin the difficult climb down to the beach, when a wild-looking man was suddenly standing in front of them, blocking their way.

'Clear off,' he bellowed. 'Get lost! This is private property. I'll set my dogs on you.' He was carrying a bockety golf umbrella with broken spokes and made a swipe at them with it. 'Ye little toe-rags. I'll have your guts for garters if ye've touched my stuff.'

The three boys scattered like fieldmice but the tramp chased after them, shouting and roaring, forcing them along the cliff and all the time taking them further away from their escape route down to the jetty and the beach. Their legs had almost given out when Liam shouted that they had shaken him off. They sank to the ground, gulping lungfuls of air.

They were on a narrow spur of land between the sea and the DART tracks. Behind them the sea cliff fell almost vertically. There was no way they could climb down there. In front of them, at the bottom of the embankment, was the black mouth of a tunnel and beyond that the railway tracks leading back to the station. As they lay there panting, their hearts pumping with fright and excitement, a northbound DART rushed out of the tunnel, its carriages emblazoned in black and gold letters with the name of a new chocolate bar. They watched it as it headed down the track towards the next station. A couple of minutes later a southbound train came towards them, this time in the usual DART livery of apple green, and disappeared into the tunnel.

'How frequent are they?' said Marcus.

'What do you mean?' asked Liam.

'How often do the trains come?'

'I'm not sure. About every five minutes.'

'You know that we're going to have to run through that tunnel,' said Marcus.

'No,' said Liam. The thought of making his tired mother angry flashed through his mind.

'Posh Boy is right, Liam,' said Thomas. 'It's the only way to get home. We can't go back the way we came with that looper at the folly blocking us off from the steps.'

'No!' said Liam. 'We'll just wait a while for him to go away.'

'Don't be stupid,' Thomas exploded. 'He lives there. He's not going to go away. He knows it was us who wrecked his things.'

No one spoke for a while. At last Marcus turned to Thomas.

'I dare you,' he said.

'I dare you first,' said Thomas.

'Double dare you,' said Marcus.

Liam was chewing his bottom lip. 'OK.' He stood up. 'We'll all do it. But we have to do it together, at the same time.'

*

They slithered down the embankment, through the bracken, the scratchy black-berry bushes, the mud-spattered news-papers, the drink cans, old trainers and all the rest of the junk that people throw out of the trains. When they reached the bottom they stood at the side of the tracks. They nervously eyed the black hole of the tunnel, then swivelled round to see if anything was coming from the opposite direction. One southbound train passed. Then a couple of minutes later the northbound approached, its horn blasting away.

'Right,' said Marcus when the back of the last carriage had vanished into the tunnel, 'on the count of three. One, two, three. GO!'

They were off like rockets, running in single file into the mouth of the tunnel. Immediately they were plunged into pitch blackness and the foul smell of dirt and diesel and grease. Because of the way the tunnel curved, they couldn't see light at the far end, and because of the darkness, they couldn't see the tracks, so they kept tripping over the rails and sleepers. They couldn't see one another very well either, but each heard the stumbling and sniffing and fast breathing of the others.

'Stop,' Marcus shouted. His voice echoed

back at him in the cavernous gloom. 'We ought to stick together.'

Thomas and Liam groped their way towards him and they moved off again in a single row, arms round each other's shoulders. A flash of light briefly lit up one wall of the tunnel and some way off there was a rumble that might have been the sea.

'Great,' said Thomas, 'we must be getting near the end.'

Another, stronger flash of light hit the tunnel wall.

'Holy God,' shouted Liam, making a flying leap off to one side. 'Watch out, there's a train coming.'

A blast of hot air seemed to suck the last breath out of the tunnel and suddenly a train was bearing down upon them, headlamps full on. Liam, Thomas and Marcus pressed themselves hard against the greasy black wall, their mouths open in a silent scream. As the engine drew nearer, they caught a glimpse of the horrified face of the driver, gesturing at them to keep clear of the tracks. Carriage after carriage flashed past, a blur of shapes and faces and colours, like a film being fast-forwarded. They pressed themselves harder against the wall, wishing they could shrink, become invisible.

The instant the last carriage had passed

they broke into a run and, with hearts racing, burst into the bright light of the afternoon. Coughing and retching, they scrambled up the other embankment and dropped exhausted to their knees.

'Omigod,' gasped Thomas, at last. 'I thought I was going to wet myself.'

Marcus turned to him. 'Do I look as terrible as you two?'

The three of them inspected each other, gravely noting their filthy, frightened faces, their tangled hair, their scratched and bleeding legs, their grimy clothes.

'Yes,' they answered together. And all three threw themselves into a bear hug, holding on to each other as they collapsed in a heap of laughter and sobs of relief. Then they took to their heels, running and running as if their lives depended on it, until they came to a gap in the railway wall and were able to squeeze their way through into a back lane behind a row of terraced houses. Again they broke into a run and didn't even stop when they reached the familiar dog-leg of the High Street. They charged on, banging into prams, knocking things out of people's arms.

'Lads, lads,' a man shouted angrily, grabbing at the back of Thomas's jacket.

They ran past Eddie Rockets and its tasty

smell of hamburger and fried onions, they ran past The Big Bad Wolf where Liam's dad was probably pulling pints for Riverdancers and dotcom millionaires, they ran past the Romanian man selling *The Big Issues*.

At Marcus's front door, they stopped.

'Will you tell?' asked Thomas, grabbing his sleeve.

Marcus shook his head.

'Swear!' said Liam.

'I swear,' said Marcus solemnly. 'But you have to swear too.'

'I swear,' said Thomas.

'I swear,' said Liam.

They nodded at each other and grinned.

'See ya,' said Liam, moving off.

Marcus had turned to put the key in the lock when there was a whistle behind him.

'Hey, Posh Boy,' Thomas shouted over his shoulder. 'That was deadly. See you on Monday.'

GIANTS
OF THE SUN

Sam McBratney

Matt's trouble with the giants began one Monday afternoon in his grandfather's house.

He often called in to see Grandpa on the way home from school. Usually Matt found him sitting alone in a room with only one window, maybe smoking his pipe or tapping at the computer, but more often just thinking. Matt had no idea what he might be thinking about, because you could never tell what was happening inside another person's head. Mum guessed that he sometimes thought about Granny, who had died five or six years ago. Ages ago.

When Matt came in, the first thing Grandpa did was make him a big sandwich. He would use a whole banana or three or four squares of cooked ham or half a box of lovely sweet dates. Very often the round of bread was cut neatly into triangles, but Grandpa didn't believe in chopping off the crusts. He said it was good for you to chew.

While crawling under the kitchen table that Monday afternoon, Matt came face to face with one of his grandfather's empty walking boots. It was so huge that Matt couldn't imagine how his own wee foot would ever fit such a thing. It made him feel small just to look at it. *The boots of a giant must be like that*, he thought, *only far bigger*. A giant's foot might be the size of a house. Or even a football pitch.

That was the start of him thinking about giants. How real are they? he wondered on the way home from Grandpa's. Is a giant less real than . . . a *panda*? He didn't know. The only giants he'd ever seen were on the TV screen or in books, but then the same was true of pandas. And what if he himself never grew very much, but always stayed small in the world?

None of that would have mattered if a bad dream hadn't come in the night and really scared him. In the dream, two giants marched across an open space to fight one another. The earth shook with the thump of their feet – feet bound up in sacks and tied round the ankles with string. It all seemed so clear to him! He saw every wrinkle in each ugly face, and he saw, too, the ginger colour of their beards. They stood so high that they could reach into the passing clouds, from where they fetched arrows of ice; and these arrows they shot at one another until Matt woke up, clutching at the covers and crying strange wee cries, like whimpers.

His mother came into the room, rushing. 'Would you look at the state of you!' she said.

Matt breathed slowly out and in and tried to make his mouth smile. He told her about the bit of trouble he was having with giants in his thoughts. Were they real? How much was a giant less real than a panda, for he'd never seen either one?

'Than a *panda*?' echoed his mother, giving him a squeeze. 'Dear child, I don't know what you're talking about. Och, you're far too easily frightened by things, they're not real.'

'But how could I see them so well? What about the arrows of ice?'

His mother shook her head as she sighed. 'We'll have to leave your light on the night. Sure, nobody makes arrows from ice . . .'

In school next day, Matt asked his friends Danielle and Hugh if they were a bit afraid of giants. Danielle, who was impressively tall, said that she wasn't.

'I might be if I actually saw a *real* one,' said Hugh.

'I've seen two,' Matt told them. 'They shot arrows at one another – arrows made of ice. It was in a dream.'

'Dreams aren't real life!' said Danielle;

and Hugh slowly shook his head as if to agree that a giant in a dream didn't truly count.

On that Tuesday afternoon Matt called to see his grandfather again, and this time the sandwiches were sardine sandwiches. Grandpa sat in a round-backed chair – it was called a captain's chair – watching him eat. They talked about sardines for a while, and then, because sardines were fish, Grandpa went on to mention a monster salmon he'd almost caught one time in the river Lee; only he didn't catch it because the fish came off the hook at the last second and got clean away.

'If only I'd had a net with me,' said Grandpa, 'I could have scooped him in.'

'Would it still be alive today, that fish you didn't catch?' Matt asked him.

'Oh, I doubt it, I was young then. Mind you, salmon can live for a brave few years.'

After a quiet moment in their talking, Matt said, 'Mummy says I'm too easily frightened.'

'Oh, aye?'

Matt told him then about the giants. He described his dream, and the curious sense he sometimes had of feeling small in the world. Also, he mentioned the arrows of ice. His grandfather listened without speaking.

'Are *you* afraid of anything?' Matt asked him.

'Me? I suppose I am.'

What of? Matt couldn't help wondering. Getting old, maybe. He could see for himself that his grandfather wasn't young any more, and for a moment he thought how strange it was that people run out of time, like one of those egg-timer things running out of sand.

'Are you afraid of dying, like Granny did?'

Grandpa chuckled, although Matt didn't see what was funny. 'That doesn't bother me much. I don't think so, anyway.'

'What then?'

'It's not easy to explain. You see, you're afraid of different things at different times of your life.'

'Like what?' said Matt.

'All sorts of things.'

'You mean to do with money?'

'No, it needn't be money, *wee* things! If you knew what frightens me now you'd say, *that's* a stupid thing to be scared of.'

'But like what?' Matt persisted.

With a sort of groan his grandfather shifted in the captain's chair so that he sat up very straight. 'Well all right, I'll tell you something that frightens me at my age. Buying flowers. That's between you and me, a sort of a secret. I'd like to buy some roses for a friend of mine and it's not easy. There.'

'I don't see what's scary about buyin' flowers.'

'She might not want them. I might seem like a fool, an old fool.'

'How?'

'It's hard to explain,' said Grandpa, raising his voice a little. 'I told you, didn't I, that bein' afraid is a funny thing and you wouldn't understand? I think we'll change the subject.' Then he jabbed a pointy finger at Matt. 'Just remember that everybody's afraid of something – you don't let it get you down, that's all. Now come on, it's filling the dishwasher time.' Grandpa called it 'filling the dishwasher' but actually they hardly ever filled it because he didn't use enough dishes or pots.

Just before Matt set off for home, his grandfather grinned down at him and said without any warning, 'Ireland's comin' down with giants, you know. The place is full o' them.'

'How do you know?'

'I've seen them.'

'What?'

'Oh, aye. With this pair of eyes I have seen the giants of the sun, and a mighty tribe they are, too. They can be five times, six times, *ten* times longer than me.' He bent down, and lowered his voice almost to a whisper. 'And you've seen them too.'

'I haven't seen them, Grandpa.'

'I tell you what – come round tomorrow afternoon and I'll tell you all about them. Right?'

'OK.'

That night Matt's daddy carried him up the stairs on his shoulders, dumped him into bed from a good height, and then tucked him in. 'On or off tonight?' he said, with a finger on the light switch.

'On, please. Daddy, Grandpa says he's seen giants.'

'Has he? Well *I* say your grandpa has no more seen a ghost than the rest of us.'

'Not a ghost, *giants*. The giants of the sun. They're twenty times bigger than a human, Daddy, and they're absolutely *huge*. Have you never seen them?'

'I have not and neither has he. Ghosts, giants, spooks, there's none of them real, nor vampires and zombies either, so go to your sleep!'

Matt's brain told him that his daddy was probably right – for some reason there happened to be a strange collection of made-up things that didn't actually exist in the world, and giants were part of all that. And yet he wondered about those arrows of ice.

Where did *they* come from? In all his life he'd never heard of such things before, so how did he think them up in his sleep?

Also, he wondered who the giants of the sun might be . . .

When Matt called at his grandfather's house on Wednesday there was someone else there – a lady visitor. She and Grandpa were drinking tea out of small cups with gold rims. A nice green cloth lay over the table, and on the cloth sat a thing with three layers: a top plate for buns, a middle plate for shortbread and a large bottom plate for sandwiches. The sandwiches had been cut into triangles and Matt noticed something else about them: no crusts.

'Mrs Cunningham, this is my grandson Matt. Say hello to Mrs Cunningham, Matt.'

Matt said hello, and so did Mrs Cunningham. She looked quite bright and shiny in the room, probably because her clothes were mainly red, like her lips.

'It's very nice to meet you, Matt,' she said. 'I'm your grandfather's friend.'

For a while Mrs Cunningham wanted to hear what he had done in school today; then she began to talk to Grandpa about next Saturday's jumble sale in the church hall – would they have enough stuff, would it be any good and what should they charge for things?

His grandfather seemed a bit different this afternoon. He talked quite a lot and laughed more than usual. After a while Matt could see that Mrs Cunningham would be here for some time, so he might as well go home.

'I'll call in tomorrow and hear about the giants, Grandpa,' Matt said, and up went Mrs Cunningham's eyebrows.

'Giants?' she said loudly, pretending to be amazed. Matt could hear them laughing as he left.

That night's homework didn't take too long, so Matt was able to help his mother look out some things for the church sale on Saturday. He found some good books that other children might want to read, and also some toys that he didn't use any more.

'All they need is batteries to make them work,' he pointed out.

'I am not buying batteries, Matt,' said his mother. 'Your grandpa can buy batteries if he wants to, this is all for him.'

'And Mrs Cunningham too,' Matt said.

His mother stopped shoving things into a black plastic bag. 'I beg your pardon? How do *you* know Mrs Cunningham?'

'I saw her round at Grandpa's house having tea, she calls him Jim.'

Now his mother sat back on her heels as if this demanded attention. 'Ethel Cunningham was in your grandfather's house, having tea?'

'In those proper wee cups he keeps in the cabinet. She's Grandpa's friend.'

'I know she is,' his mother said, a bit sharply.

'Mummy, if Grandpa bought somebody roses, how could he look like an old fool?'

'Roses?'

For a while Matt thought his mother wouldn't say any more. A deep frown had appeared at the top of her nose, which often happened when she thought a lot. Or got cross. Maybe she didn't want Grandpa to have a friend like Mrs Cunningham, although Matt couldn't see why not.

'Why, did he say he was going to buy roses for someone?'

'No, he said it was a thing you would be really afraid to do if you were his age. He'd rather meet a *giant* than buy flowers.'

'Well he's right, you can't just buy flowers for whoever you like and it is very possible to look foolish.' Then his mother closed her eyes for a moment, and muttered, 'Whatever next . . . ?'

On Thursday, by a coincidence, Matt's teacher read out a story about a giant. He lived high in the lonely mountains and only woke up every hundred years or so, therefore very few people knew about him. At the end of the story Matt asked his teacher if she had ever seen a giant with her own eyes. She replied that she hadn't.

'My grandpa has seen giants, Miss McCracken.'

'Oh? Would that be recently, Matt?'

'Yes I think so, he says Ireland's full of them and he's going to show them to me soon.'

There was a pause, followed by a quick smile from Miss McCracken. 'Well, you must remember to tell me and the class all about that when it happens.' Then she told everyone to set out their topic books and there was no more talk about giants.

Afterwards, coming home from school, Danielle said that Miss McCracken probably thought Matt's grandad was mad. 'Do you think Hugh and me could meet him?' she asked slyly.

'Then we could tell people that we know a man who's seen giants,' said Hugh.

'No,' said Matt. 'And he's not mad.'

Things were back to normal at his grandfather's house when Matt arrived there – no green cloth, no fancy cups, no Mrs Cunningham. Grandpa made him cheese sandwiches cut into squares and with crusts for chewing, all washed down with milk from a tall glass.

'Will you tell me now about the giants of the sun, Grandpa?' Matt said when he'd finished eating.

'I'll do better than that. I think I can show them to you. Come on out the back.'

The day was bright and blowy. From the latch door Matt and his grandfather looked across the garden to the whitewashed walls of some garages beyond. Nothing much grew in the garden, for it was still early spring and sometimes a withering frost came in the night. The raspberry canes stood there like bare sticks. It was hard to believe that summer would come and fill them with lovely fruit again.

'There they are,' said Grandpa, waving a hand. 'The giants of the sun. Yours and mine, we've got one each. Look at the length of them!'

But not a thing could Matt see between himself and the garages beyond. Then he noticed the movement of a large dark head – his own – against the white of the far wall, and of course he guessed.

'You mean *shadows*,' he cried. 'It's a trick!'

'It's not a trick. You can see the giants and

they're made by the sun. You can't deny that I've shown you the giants of the sun, now, can you?'

They're not very scary giants, Matt thought. He wondered whether that trick would work on Miss McCracken.

'Mind you,' his grandfather was saying, 'all giants are the same. See in there?' he tapped Matt on the head. 'That's where they live, in there.'

'You mean there aren't any real ones.'

'None. Never was, never will be unless they live on some planet way out in space.'

'But what about the arrows of ice, Grandpa?'

'Made up, by your very own head. 'Tis a grand idea, though – "arrows of ice".'

At that moment Matt's grandpa was standing by the latch door, watching his whirligig of washing turning slowly in the breeze, shirt-tails and their shadows. He seemed full of lightness today as he sang a bit of a song.

'Do you know what I did this morning? You'd never guess what I did. I bought something.'

'Did you buy some flowers?' asked Matt.

It was a good guess. His grandfather glanced down at him in mighty surprise, and then he smiled.

'Boys, you are one quare fella,' he said, suddenly swooping Matt up and holding him high.

COLIN OF THE FOLEYS

Stephanie Dagg

Colin didn't want to go into the tunnel. He was scared. But the rest of his class were cheerfully disappearing into it and Colin didn't want to be the only wimp.

'Come on, Colin, you big drip,' jeered Gavin as he dropped down into the darkness.

Colin swallowed hard. To take his mind off the black hole at his feet, he looked around him at the reconstructed ring fort that they had come to visit on their school tour. The fort itself was a big, circular house with wattle and daub walls and a roof woven from sticks. There were some smaller buildings too and, surrounding everything, a tall wooden fence that had a walkway at the top. They'd just gone round that. It had been brilliant, gazing out over the fence and imagining what it must have been like, a thousand years ago, to be on watch for enemies.

Now the fun was over, though. Now they had to go down into the black hole and crawl through the tunnel. In the past, the tunnel had been used to escape from the fort if it fell into enemy hands. But it had also been used to hide the women and children if enemies attacked, to stop them being taken as slaves. Colin had been shocked when the two guides working at the ring fort had told them that there had once been a brisk trade in slaves in Ireland. Colin wondered what he would have done had he been there then – trapped between the enemy and his fear of the cold, dark space.

Colin's eyes were drawn back to the tiny entrance. There were just two people in front of him now. It was decision time. Should he go in or should he admit, in front of everyone, that he was afraid? He groaned. It was no good. He'd *have* to go in. His classmates would never stop teasing him if he backed out now. And anyway, he was all prepared, with his knee pads, elbow pads and hard hat. He sighed.

'In you go!' said one of the guides cheerfully. The other had gone in first with a torch to show the way. This guide was staying outside to roll the big stone slab back over the entrance once the last person – Colin – had gone in. Colin's hands began to sweat. He felt a bit dizzy. He must have looked pale because the guide smiled at him and said, 'Are you OK? You know, you don't have to go in. I don't like it in there much, either. That's why I volunteered to stay outside.'

'I'm fine, thanks,' said Colin in a wobbly voice, thinking of the others and of Gavin's sneers. 'I'll go.'

Slowly, very slowly, he lowered himself into the hole. He dropped down to the bottom, then crouched, ready to crawl along the passageway. It was small and dark and tiny. He could just make out the last person's bottom and feet, disappearing in front of him. 'Hey, wait for me!' he croaked.

'Come on then, slowcoach,' he heard Gavin laugh.

But Colin couldn't hurry. His arms and legs felt as though they were made of concrete. He could hardly move. *Come on, you great coward*, he told himself. *You'll get left behind.*

That was an awful thought. What if he *did* get left behind? What if the guide at the other end sealed the exit before he got there? There was a stone over that end too. What if everyone forgot he was still in there? Colin shuffled forward as quickly as he could. His rucksack bounced uncomfortably on his back and he kept clipping his head on the tunnel roof. Even with a hard hat on, it hurt. His heart was beating at a million miles an hour. He had to get out.

Suddenly, in the gloom, Colin saw that the

passageway in front of him split into two. The guide had said that this had been done to confuse any enemies who might get in. The family would know the way out, but the enemies wouldn't. With any luck they'd go down the dead end and get stuck, giving the family time to get out. And Colin couldn't see which way Gavin had gone.

'Help!' he squeaked. His mouth was so dry he hardly made a sound. He felt sick with panic. *Oh no, don't let me throw up in the tunnel, in the cold and the dark.* It already smelled bad enough in there, sort of musty and a bit cabbagey. He was just about to turn round and crawl back the way he'd come when he heard the crunch of the big stone being heaved back over the entrance. What little light there had been vanished. Colin froze.

Then his eye picked up a flicker of light down the passageway that went to the left. Now Colin felt sick with relief. He launched himself after that glimmer. He just wanted to catch up with the others and get out of this nightmare place. At last he could see daylight streaming into the tunnel ahead of him. But, to his horror, it began to dim. Someone was closing the exit! Too stunned to shout a protest, Colin hurtled towards the stone. He got there just as it was sliding into place. He stuck his hands into the small gap and heaved with all his might. 'Let me out,' he yelled. 'This isn't funny!'

The stone slid away and Colin began to climb up towards freedom. In his frantic effort, he knocked his hard hat down over his eyes. He couldn't see anything now. But he could feel, and he stopped dead. A cold blade pushed against his throat. Suddenly he felt anger. This was going way too far! It was probably a joke they played on the last person out of the tunnel – first pretending to shut him in and then pretending to be an enemy ambushing him as he came out. Some joke.

'Give me a break!' he shouted, grabbing at the hand holding the knife to his neck. He pushed it away and at the same time pushed his hard hat back into place. He turned his head and glared at his would-be attacker, expecting it to be the guide who had led them through the tunnel. He also expected to see the rest of his class sniggering at him. But he didn't see them. Instead he saw two scared-looking girls and a thin boy about his own age. The boy was holding a small, iron knife. One of the girls held a glowing stick from a fire, a sort of torch. They were dressed in woollen clothes, the girls wearing long tunics with pinafore-like dresses over them and the boy a baggy top and breeches. They looked very much like the clothes that Colin had seen on display in the ring fort, as examples of the garments people wore at the time that it was built. They must be child actors, Colin decided, who worked here during the summer to make it seem more real. It was their job to play this nasty trick on whoever was last out of the tunnel.

He looked around wildly, trying to spot where his friends were hiding. He couldn't see them anywhere. Instead he felt the hairs on the back of his neck stand up and a cold chill trickle down his spine. There were a lot of trees around him. When they'd been up on the walkway, the guide had pointed to where the escape tunnel came out – and there hadn't been a tree in sight. In fact, there had hardly been anything leafy growing around the ring fort. It had been surrounded by fallow farmland. Colin looked back at the fort. That looked different too. The fence around it was a darker colour and seemed to be taller. And Colin couldn't hear the sound of traffic in the distance.

Feeling very wobbly, he scrambled out of the tunnel. He faced the three children who were gazing at him, mouths open, and suddenly he realized: he hadn't just travelled along the terrifying tunnel, he had travelled back in time!

But how? Clearly the children had never seen anyone in twenty-first-century clothes before. 'It's just a boy! It can't be an enemy!' gasped one of the girls. Colin could just about understand what she was saying. She was speaking Irish, but with a strong accent that he didn't recognize.

'Of course I'm not an enemy,' he replied as calmly as he could, one eye on the knife.

'I'm not so sure,' growled the boy, advancing. 'How come he chased us through the tunnel?'

'Donal, he's the same age as you!' said the other girl. 'Even enemies don't send children to fight. He must be a slave. They must have had some prisoners with them when they attacked our fort. He must be trying to escape from them, like us. *Are* you a slave?' she asked Colin.

Colin thought about all the extra jobs he'd been doing around the house lately for Mum since his baby sister had been born. 'Yes, I'm a slave all right.'

The boy lowered his knife, and he and the girls approached Colin cautiously. One of the girls tapped the hard hat.

'I have never seen such clothes,' she marvelled. 'What clan are you from?'

What does she mean? thought Colin. *Clan?* Then his brain cleared. 'Oh, what *family*, you mean? I'm a Foley.'

'I have never heard of Foleys,' she said, shaking her head. 'You must have come a long way.'

If only you knew, thought Colin.

'I'm Brigid,' the girl smiled. 'And this is my sister Orla and my brother Donal.'

'This is no time to talk,' said Donal. 'Quickly, we must hide. Follow me.'

He disappeared into the trees and led the others to a small thicket of dense, prickly bushes.

'In there,' he ordered. 'You'll be safe. I'll be back in a minute.'

'Where are you going?' asked Colin. He didn't want Donal to leave with their only weapon, especially if there were attackers around.

'I'm going back to the fort to see what's happening. Mother and Father are still there.'

'Be careful,' pleaded Brigid.

'I will. Don't worry,' promised Donal. He hurried off.

Donal seemed to be gone for ages, but Colin didn't want to risk checking his watch. How would he explain what it was to the girls?

Just when the girls were beginning to look desperate and Colin was wondering if he should go after Donal, a rustling in the bushes announced his return. His eyes were shining with excitement.

'There are only two enemies in the fort at the moment,' he told them. 'They're guarding Mother and Father, who are tied up in the cowshed.'

'Where are the others?' asked Brigid. 'At least five enemies attacked us.'

'They're probably hunting for us,' replied Donal. Colin shuddered. 'So now is a good time to get back into the fort.'

'Is it?' Colin couldn't see why.

'It's poorly guarded at the moment. You and I will have to attack the two enemies while the girls untie Mother and Father.'

'What?'

'You ask many questions,' said Donal crossly. 'Are you afraid?'

'No,' said Colin quickly. He thought of the tunnel, of how scared he'd felt inside it. But he'd gone through it, he'd faced his fears. 'No,' he repeated. 'I don't think I am.'

'I have my knife,' said Donal. 'Do you have a weapon?'

Colin was about to shake his head, but then he thought of something. He smiled. 'Actually, I've got quite a few. I'll show you.'

Ten minutes later the four of them were crouched outside the ring-fort fence.

'There is a hidden gate here,' Donal told them, gently pulling at the bottom of two of the posts. 'Father showed me it once. It's another way of escaping in case we couldn't get to the tunnel. It's lucky for us that it's just behind the cowshed.'

He eased two short pieces of wood out of the way. 'Everyone know what to do?'

'We do,' nodded Brigid.

'Here goes then. Good luck!' Donal vanished into the compound. Brigid and Orla followed, then last of all, Colin. The girls crept behind the cowshed, armed with Donal's knife to cut the ropes binding their parents. Colin and Donal moved stealthily round to the side, armed with very different weapons. They peered round the wall. Sitting in front of them were the two attackers. Colin was relieved by how unscary they looked. He'd been imagining hairy, angry giants. Instead he saw two small, scruffy men. He was a match for them!

Donal tapped on the wall. One attacker looked up. Donal tapped again.

'What's that?' asked the man.

'We'd better have a look,' said his friend nervously.

They got up and walked gingerly towards the boys' hiding place.

'Now!' hissed Donal. He and Colin leaped out in front of the men, shouting and sticking out tongues that were vivid orange, thanks to Colin's brightly-coloured boiled sweets that they'd just been sucking. The enemies halted in alarm. Donal brought his fist crashing down on the empty, inflated crisp packet he was holding. The bang made the men jump back. Colin gave his can of Coke one last hard shake, then pulled off the tab and sprayed it into the attackers' faces. They gave a roar and dropped their swords. They rubbed madly at their stinging eyes. One of them fell to his knees. Colin pounced forward and pushed him down. Then he dug into his pocket for his portable CD player. He'd already switched it on. He turned the volume button to its highest setting and shoved the earphones over the attacker's head. The man shrieked in fear and pain. Donal, meanwhile, had picked up one of the swords and was using it to pin the other enemy against the wall. With his free hand, he was holding Colin's Gameboy under the man's nose. The flashing lights and music that were part of the game running on it terrified him.

'What sorcery is this?' he gasped.

'There's no sorcery here!' thundered a voice behind Colin. He swung round in alarm. A tall, strong man stood there, armed with an evil-looking axe.

Crikey, thought Colin. *Now we're for it.*

But Donal grinned. 'Father!' he called happily.

Donal's father strode over to his son, grabbed the enemy by his hair and whacked him on the head with his axe handle. The man fell silently to the ground. Then Donal's father turned to deal with Colin's attacker. He looked curiously at Colin, who quickly got out of his way.

'Thanks indeed for helping my family,' he said, reaching towards the attacker. 'Fetch ropes, Donal. We'll tie these men up.'

By now Orla and Brigid had reappeared with their mother. The woman looked shaken. And the sight of Colin didn't help to calm her down.

'It's all right, Mother,' laughed Orla. 'He's a Foley from a long way away. They dress strangely and they have some funny weapons. Show Mother, Colin.'

But before Colin could move, there was a loud thudding at the main gate. Colin's heart lurched. He wasn't sure how many more frights he could take today.

Donal's father finished tying up the

prisoners and grabbed his axe again. He raced to the gate. 'Who's there?' he bellowed.

'It's Ryan O'Neill and his brothers,' came a voice.

'Enter, friends.' Donal's father unlocked the gate and swung it open. Four tall men came in, dragging three others behind them.

'We were hunting close by and came across these fellows,' smiled Ryan. 'They didn't give us much trouble. And with a bit of persuasion they soon told us that they had attacked your fort. We came to help but it seems that you have already sorted the matter out!'

'Thanks, neighbour. We had some help from an escaped slave,' Donal's father told him. 'You must meet this boy. He is the strangest-looking imp. Donal? Where's your friend? Donal?'

But Donal and Colin were nowhere to be seen. In fact, they were crouched down close to the entrance to the tunnel.

'Must you go?' asked Donal.

'Yes,' nodded Colin. 'Your family is safe now. It's just too difficult for me to try to explain who I am and where I've come from.'

'Why? Haven't you told us the truth, then?' said Donal. 'Aren't you really an escaped slave?'

Colin shook his head. 'No. Look, it sounds crazy I know, but I've come from the future. My school, that is, me and my friends, will visit your fort in a thousand years' time. I'll go through the tunnel here, but somehow I don't come out with my friends, I come out and bump into you and your sisters. And then we fight the enemies and stuff.'

Donal looked at him closely. Then he nodded. 'I believe you, Colin. I mean, your clothes and your weapons, they're not from our time. And I don't believe they're sorcery either.' He grinned. 'So you think if you go through the tunnel again you will arrive back in your own time?'

'Well, I hope so,' shrugged Colin. 'I can't think of any other way to get back. And now seems like a good time, while your father is busy with those people.'

'I understand,' Donal smiled. 'But I will miss you, Colin of the Foleys. You are a brave and cunning warrior.'

Colin thought for a moment and then grinned. 'Yes, I suppose I am, aren't I.'

Together the two boys heaved away the big stone covering the entrance. Colin took a deep breath and looked into the dark tunnel. This time there was no torch to light the way. *I can do it*, he thought to himself.

I've fought vicious raiders, I can do this. And, somehow, he knew he would be all right.

'Good luck, friend,' said Donal.

'Good luck, friend,' replied Colin. He gave Donal a thumbs-up sign. Donal looked puzzled for a moment, then stuck his own thumb up too. Colin slid down into the tunnel for the second time that day.

And this time it was a lot easier.

After all, this time Colin of the Foleys, brave and cunning warrior, was going home.

THE Y GIRLS

Siobhán Parkinson

My name's Khyley Doyle. It used to be Kyley Doyle, but I added the H in to make it more mysterious-looking. You need something a bit different if you are going to be on the telly.

My dad freaked out when he saw the new spelling. I don't know, I think it must be because of giving up the smokes. It makes him terrible cranky. He said my name was bad enough to start with, too many Ys, and what was wrong with Mary? That is typical of my dad, he'll say something completely out of nowhere and you're supposed to treat it as if it is logical.

But that isn't the point of this story. The point is that me and my two best friends Kelsey and Chelsey were going to be a girl band. Mind you, it took a bit of persuading to get them interested in the idea.

'What *about* a girl band?' This was Kelsey. She's always picking holes in things.

'We can *be* one!' I said. 'We have lovely voices. The choir teacher said so.'

'Us?' asked Chelsey.

'Yeah, us!' I said. 'We're naturals. I don't know why I didn't think of it sooner.'

'Would we be on telly?' asked Kelsey.

'Of course we'd be on telly. Where else would we be? We'd be famous.'

'Would we be rich?' said Chelsey.

'Zillionaires,' I said. 'Look at Britney Spears.'

'She isn't a girl band,' said Kelsey.

'Same difference,' I said. 'She sings, doesn't she? And that one with the screechy voice, you know, and the really smooth hair. She makes a fortune. I read about her in the paper.'

'But she's a proper singer,' said Kelsey. 'She sings holy songs. We don't know any holy songs.'

'It doesn't matter,' I said. 'The point is, if she can do it, why can't we?'

'My ma thinks she's great.' This was Chelsey, banging on about your one with the really smooth hair, who sings the holy songs.

'She wears sparkly eyeshadow,' added Kelsey.

I thought that was interesting. That'd be an added bonus to being rich and famous and on the telly.

'We'll get some,' I said.

'We wouldn't be *let* wear sparkly eyeshadow,' Kelsey argued.

'Not in a fit,' said Chelsey.

'We would if we were famous,' I said. 'But anyway, if you'd rather I went ahead and had a brilliant career as a singer all by myself, that's fine with me. Forget I asked.'

That shook them.

'Would we get to meet boy bands?' asked Kelsey.

'Definitely,' I said.

'OK so,' they said together.

They're hard work, sometimes, those two, but in the end they usually do give in.

'What'll we wear?' I said. I knew that'd keep them interested in the idea. They're both big into clothes.

We didn't have any money for proper girl-band clothes, so we tried putting a bit of colouredy net that we pinched off Kelsey's little sister's green tutu – the one she wore when she was being a Christmas tree in the school play – over a black leotard and tights. But the effect wasn't really what we'd had in mind. Maybe the colour was wrong. The black leotard's still a good idea, and you could try a metallic waistcoat with it. Or leopardskin.

Chelsey is sometimes very creative, I'll give her that. She was the one who thought of calling us Girl Power on Wheels.

'Yes,' said Kelsey, suddenly getting enthusiastic. 'And we can wear roller skates.'

'Or come on stage on those little scooters,' I said. 'We'd be the only girl band that scoots on stage in leotards.'

'Or The Scooters,' said Kelsey. 'We could call ourselves The Scooters.'

Only none of us has a scooter. We haven't got any roller skates either, come to think of it.

'We could always drop the skates anyway,' I said, 'or the scooters, if we couldn't afford them, and call ourselves The Y Girls, since we all have Ys in our names. The Y Girls.'

'That's what I've been asking myself for years,' said Lee. He's my brother, a troublemaker pure and simple. I don't know where he sprang up out of, but he's always around when you don't want him. '"Why girls? Why does God bother?" I ask myself.'

'You stupid eejit,' I said. 'Y, not *Why*.'

'You all have Ls in your names too,' he said. 'You might as well call it The L Girls.' He nearly burst himself laughing, he thought that was so funny. 'Ha-ha, ha-ha! L-L – The Hell Girls! That'd be a great name.'

I slammed the door of the shed in his face. That's where we were practising, my dad's garden shed. We're not really allowed in there because he says it's dangerous. It's full of rusty old nails and dusty old bicycle tyres (even though nobody in our house has a bicycle) and a bent-looking saw and a hammer or two, but the main thing is an old radio that he has. It's supposed to be broken, but it works perfectly well because I often hear the races coming out of the shed on a Saturday afternoon. You know it's the races because the man shrieks in that breathless way, a bit like your one with the smooth hair, when you come to think of it. There must be money in shrieking. People seem to be doing it all over the shop and getting paid for it.

Anyway, we weren't shrieking, we were singing nice and tunefully, even though we were freezing in the shed with only leotards and tights on. We had sparkly eyeshadow on too, Chelsey had lifted it from her older sister's bedroom, but that doesn't help much against the cold.

We thought we'd start with cover versions, because we haven't got much experience with writing songs. The only thing was, we didn't have any instruments or a backing group or anything, so we sounded a bit thin when we started singing. But then I had another brilliant idea.

'Let's find a pop station on the radio!' I said. 'And we can sort of karaoke along to a few things, just for practice, just till we think up some way of getting music.'

That worked great, as I knew it would, and we warmed up after a while because we did dancing as well. We really were shaping up great. I *knew* it was a fantastic idea, and I could see we were going to be mega. At least I was. The others were just OK.

The only problem was money. It's not enough to sound fabulous and look gorgeous, like we do. You have to do demo tapes and pay sound engineers and get a manager and everything if you are planning to go on the telly. There's always the Lotto, but you have to be eighteen to play it, and we didn't want to wait that long. Chelsey said why didn't we go on *Who Wants to Be a Millionaire?* It's a clever name for a programme, isn't it, because, of course, everyone in the whole world wants to be a millionaire, but when you think of all the hassle, having to phone a friend and the whole country listening to you, I don't think it's worth it.

That's what I said to Chelsey anyway, and she was a bit miffed, so I said, 'Well, OK, then, Chel, why don't *you* go on it? See if you like it.' After that she was even more miffed. There's no pleasing some people, is there?

Then I had this really brill idea about day-old chicks. They cost half-nothing, you know, day-old chicks. My granda used to have them. I mean, of course, they were only day-old for a day. Then they were two days old and then three – well, you get the picture. All you have to do is mind them for a while and then they grow up into hens and start laying eggs and then you can sell the eggs and make a *fortune*. Free range, they'd be, if you let them run around in the garden, plus they could eat worms, so we wouldn't have to pay to feed them.

Thing is, though, I don't know where you get day-old chicks. The ones my granda had used to come in the post, he told me. When I told Kelsey and Chelsey that, they were horrified. They said it was like boiling lobsters. I don't know what they were on about. How could getting day-old chicks in the post be remotely like boiling lobsters?

'We'll have to go out to the country,' I said.

'The country?' they asked. 'How would we get to the country?'

I tried to think of the furthest-away place I could, where you could still go on the bus. I used to go to Enniskerry with my granda when I was small. It was pretty country, I thought.

'Enniskerry,' I said. 'One of the Rathfarnham buses goes there.'

93

'It can't,' said Kelsey. 'The Rathfarnham buses go to Rathfarnham.'

Kelsey can be a bit slow at times. '*After* Rathfarnham,' I explained. 'After Rathfarnham, it goes to Enniskerry.'

'Then it must be the Enniskerry bus,' said Kelsey. She's always arguing, that one. She always has to be right.

'Look,' I said, 'do you want to come or not?'

'Yeah,' said Kelsey.

'Yeah,' said Chelsey. 'Will we bring a packed lunch?'

I hadn't thought of that. It sounded like a good idea.

'No,' I said. (Well, it wasn't *my* idea, was it?) 'We'll get chips there.'

'Do they have chips in Enniskerry?' asked Chelsey doubtfully.

'Of course they have,' I said. 'They definitely have whipped ice cream, which means it must be civilized, so they must have chips too. Stands to reason.'

They didn't really believe me about the chips, but anyway, they were all excited about going down to the country, so we decided to go on Saturday morning after Irish dancing. We often go to the shops on Saturdays after dancing, and as long as we're together and we're home by dinner time, we're allowed. We're nearly twelve. Well, we're ten and that's nearly eleven, which is nearly twelve.

Of course, I was right about the chips. We got big bags of them and they were lovely, and then we had whipped ice cream and then it was time to go looking for day-old chicks.

Enniskerry is more towny than I remembered. Not too many farms.

'So, we'll walk,' I said. 'Up that hill and out the road a bit and there's sure to be a farm soon.'

'How do you know it'll be a chicken farm, though?' said Kelsey.

'Well, one of them is bound to be a chicken farm,' I said.

We did find a farm. At least, I think it was a farm. It was about two miles from Enniskerry and it was all fields and things around and there was a house in the middle of it, so we went and knocked on the door and asked them if they had any day-old chicks.

'No,' they said, looking a bit puzzled. Maybe it wasn't really a farmhouse.

So we walked on for a bit, and then there was another house. We were getting tired by now.

'What do you want day-old chicks for?' they asked at this house.

'To grow into free-r—' Chelsey started,

but I could see this was the wrong thing to say. These people looked the soppy sort.

'For pets!' I said quickly. 'We live in the city and we have no room for a dog, so we'd like a few chickens for pets.'

They invited us in and gave us some sort of a horrible orange drink and said we were grand girls, but they didn't have any chicks of any age and that we should think about getting a gerbil, and did our mammies know where we were?

'Of course,' I said. 'We wouldn't go anywhere without telling our parents.'

That was the right answer because they gave us fifty cents each.

'We're not supposed to take money from strangers,' said Kelsey as we ran down the hill.

'Well, it's too late now,' I said. 'What do you want to do? Go all the way up that hill again and give it back to them?'

'This was a terrible idea,' said Chelsey in her whiniest voice, 'coming out to the country. I don't like it out here and they have no chickens anyway.'

'The country has gone to pot,' I said. 'That's what's happened. I blame the telly.'

'I still think we should go on *Who Wants to Be a Millionaire?*' said Chelsey.

'We're too young,' I said. 'They wouldn't

let us. It's the same as the Lotto. There's a conspiracy against children making any money.'

'I want to go home,' said Kelsey.

That's the problem with those two. No stamina. But what can you do? I couldn't *make* them stay and try a few more farms. They'd really gone off the idea.

Of course, we were dead late home and we got into massive trouble and we were all grounded for a month. Lee was delighted.

But we were still allowed to go to each other's houses, so we went on practising for the band though, to tell you the truth, I was beginning to wonder about the other two. I wasn't sure they had what it takes to be a girl band.

One Saturday we were in the shed as usual and we were trying 'I Should Be So Lucky' and I was really giving it everything. I think I actually felt a tear trickling down my cheek where it goes on about crying in the night. Suddenly the door burst open and my dad came thundering in.

'What's going on here?' he yelled.

I bet Lee told him that we were messing around in there. I had a screwdriver in my hand. It was being a microphone. I could see Lee sniggering behind my dad with his hand over his mouth.

'That's my best screwdriver!' Dad roared. 'And what is that stuff on your eyes?'

Lee was rubbing his finger along his eyelids and making faces and pointing at us and snorting like a drain.

'And my *radio*,' said Dad. 'I'd just got that thing fixed and now you've ruined it. It's not supposed to make noises like that. It's for serious listening.'

'We only changed the station . . .' I started.

But he didn't want to know.

'Took me for ever to get it back in working order,' he was grumbling to himself. 'I'll never be able to find that station again.'

And the next thing, he reached into his toolbox and took out a packet of fags. His hands were shaking.

'DON'T DO IT!' I yelled.

'It's OK,' he said, opening the packet and burying his nose in it. 'I'm only smelling them.'

The poor man. I'd driven him to sniffing tobacco. I felt terrible.

'Here,' Dad said then, and he dug into his pocket and pulled out a big fistful of coins and poured them into my hands. 'Be off with yez, now, out of this shed and don't let me catch you next, nigh or near it again. It's dangerous in here. You might saw your-selves in half or something. Go and buy yourselves some lollipops. And if I catch you wearing that stuff on your eyes again, I'll . . . I'll . . . I'll tell your ma on you.'

I figured that 'go and buy yourselves some lollipops' meant we weren't grounded any more, but I didn't want to risk asking him so I said, 'Come on, girls, let's go.'

'Can I have some money, too, Da?' I could hear Lee asking as we scarpered up the garden.

'Sorry, son,' said Dad. He'd emptied his pockets.

We counted it in my bedroom. We'd got six euro thirty-seven cents plus a Canadian cent.

'What about the band?' said Chelsey.

'Oh, I've gone off the idea,' I said.

'But I wanted to meet boy bands,' said Kelsey.

'And I wanted to be on telly,' said Chelsey.

Really, those two, one minute they don't want anything to do with any of my ideas, girl bands or day-old chicks or going to places where there mightn't be chips, and next thing they can think of nothing else. It's time they got minds of their own.

'It's childish really,' I said, 'wanting to be a girl band. I'd rather get my voice trained and be a proper singer. And I think I'll change my name. Do you think that one who sings the holy songs uses conditioner?'

'Change your *name*?' said Chelsey, as if I had said I was going to fly to the moon or something.

'Stage name. My dad likes Mary,' I said dreamily. 'Only I'd spell it Mahry, of course, to make it more interesting. Yes, I think that would work.'

THE
SHIPWRECKED
GHOST

Gordon Snell

Orla always knew that one day her father Jimmy would marry again. It was five years now since her mother had died, when Orla was only four years old. For some time Jimmy had been going out with Rose, who worked in the same office as him. Rose wasn't the worst. And she clearly loved Orla's father very much.

So in most ways, Orla was glad for her father and for Rose and she hoped they would be happy. There was only one bad side to it all: Dekko. He was Rose's son Declan, and was a few months younger than Orla. He had spiky red hair and a loud laugh. He was a little taller than Orla, which annoyed her – but then, almost everything about Dekko annoyed her. The way he made *vroom-vroom* noises to imitate the racing cars he was so mad about. The way he cackled with laughter at the most stupid jokes and television programmes. The way he ate so quickly that his plate was empty when Orla was only halfway through her meal.

And now he and Orla were going to spend a whole week together, at this seaside place called Ballycarrig, way out on the west coast of Ireland, where her father had often spent holidays when he was a child. He and Rose had rented a house there. Orla tried to think of ways to get out of going, like pretending to be sick, or having to study for an exam, but she was such a bad liar she knew it was no good. This time next week they would be there. She would just have to 'grin and bear it'.

I'll just have to grin and bear it, thought Dekko, as he looked ahead to this holiday his mother's new man had dreamed up. Jimmy wasn't a bad guy – in fact, if he was honest, Dekko had to admit that he was a lot kinder to Dekko's mother than his own father had been. Dad was away more and more on his work trips, so it wasn't too much of a surprise when he finally said he was staying away for good, and taking up a job in another part of the country. The fact that he was also taking up with another woman wasn't mentioned, at least not in Dekko's presence. That had been three years ago, and when the divorce came through and Jimmy began to appear on the scene more and more, Dekko realized that in the end they would probably get married. That was OK with him: the only snag was Orla, who seemed to Dekko to be moody and stuck-up and only interested in reading or cooking. It was a wonder that she liked cooking, since she didn't seem to like eating: she was only ever halfway through her meal by the time Dekko had finished his. And now they were to spend a week together in this back-of-beyond place no one had ever heard of, and where there would be nothing to do except stare at the sea. Dekko yawned at the mere thought of it.

During the journey Dekko gazed out gloomily at the damp countryside where even the bright yellow flowers of the gorse on the hillsides couldn't cheer up the scene. Orla looked at the maps in a book she had, and pointed out various ruined castles or grand stone houses and read out bits about their history. Orla's father said how much better the roads had got in the past few years, and how the country looked so much more prosperous. Rose wondered how much Ballycarrig would have changed from the place Jimmy remembered as a child.

Dekko thought, when he saw the place, that it didn't look as if it had changed in the last hundred-odd years. There was a short main street with a grocery store and a souvenir shop and three pubs and a fish-and-chip shop and café. At least that was a good sign. There might be other boys hanging around there for Dekko to team up with.

Orla wondered if they could catch their own fish and cook it. She had been fishing a few times on the river with her father, and remembered the excitement of catching a fish. Maybe they could even go sea-fishing.

They left the cases in the house and all four of them walked down the path that led to the little harbour. It was like a stone horseshoe in shape, calm inside and with the sea churning outside. There were several sailing dinghies and rowing boats in the harbour. On the quay sat a bearded man in a navy leather jacket and jeans, with rubber boots. He was fiddling with some basket-like objects with netting over them.

'Those are for catching lobsters,' said Orla's father, 'and that fellow I'm sure is Joe O'Brien. He used to take me out in his boat when I was a kid. Hi, Joe!' he called. The man looked up as they walked over to him.

'It's been a long time,' said Orla's father. 'And I've grown a bit since you knew me, Joe. I'm Jimmy Kenny.'

'Young Jimmy!' Joe exclaimed, shaking his hand. 'Yes, grown a bit is right!'

They were all introduced, and Joe offered to take Orla and Dekko out in the rowing boat the next day, just like he'd taken Orla's father. 'We'll go across to the island out there,' Joe said. 'Spanish Island, they call it, because of the ships from the Spanish Armada that were wrecked on the rocks.'

As they walked back to the house, Orla said, 'Imagine those ships coming all the way from Spain and crashing on to the rocks out here.'

'What were they doing here in the first place?' Dekko wondered. 'Surely the Spanish didn't take their holidays in Ballycarrig?' He laughed his cackling laugh.

'It was the Armada,' said Orla impatiently. 'The big fleet that set out to invade England, hundreds of years ago. They hit a heavy storm and were blown off course. I remember a Spanish babysitter I had. She used to talk about it, when she was trying to teach me some Spanish.'

'*I* can speak Spanish,' Dekko boasted.

'Go on then, say something,' said Orla.

Dekko roared out the football chant: '*Olé, Olé, Olé, Olé! Olé! Olé!*—'

'*Muchas gracias,*' said Orla. '*Es bastante!*'

'What's that mean?' asked Dekko.

'Thank you very much, that's enough of that!' said Orla.

'Hey, you really can speak it!' said Dekko with reluctant admiration.

Orla and Dekko sat in the stern of the boat, while Joe rowed.

'You seem to be heading away from the island,' Orla said.

'We have to go a roundabout way, because of the currents,' said Joe. 'These waters are treacherous. You need to know what you're doing.'

He brought the boat on a curving path round to the far side of the island, and rowed in to a small pebbly beach. He jumped out and tied the boat to a rock. They walked through some trees till they came to a stony headland jutting into the sea. The waves crashed on the rocks and the spray rose high into the air.

'That's where one of the ships was wrecked,' said Joe.

'Do you think any treasure was washed ashore?' asked Dekko. 'Maybe we'll discover some gold.'

'If there was any, I reckon the locals would have found it soon enough,' said Joe. 'But the story is that the ship went down and everyone was drowned, except for one young cabin-boy who swam ashore and was stranded here. He survived a few days and then died because no one found him. There are those who claim they have heard his ghost, wailing in the night wind.'

'Spooky,' said Dekko. 'I bet I know what he wailed.'

'Don't tell me,' sighed Orla, suspecting what he'd say.

Sure enough, Dekko gave a soft, eerie wail: '*Oooolé . . . Oooolé . . .*'

'You wouldn't joke if you knew all the stories,' said Joe sharply. 'Some say his voice on the wind calls out to guide passing boats to safety, but really he's guiding them to those rocks where his own ship went down.'

Dekko looked sorry for himself.

'Don't mind him,' Orla told Joe. 'He doesn't mean it. He just likes to play the eejit sometimes.'

Dekko nodded. Orla was trying to help him. Maybe she wasn't the worst, after all.

That evening over a meal of fish and chips, Orla said, 'Maybe we can catch our own fish, Dad, and cook it.'

'Yes, I've brought a fishing rod,' said her father. 'Why don't you bring it with you tomorrow? Perhaps Joe will take you out in the boat again.'

*

The next morning Orla and Dekko walked down to the harbour, but there was no sign of Joe. There were no lobster pots on the quay, either.

'He must be out at sea, laying the pots,' said Orla.

'But the rowing boat's there,' said Dekko.

'He probably uses a bigger boat for the lobster pots,' Orla said. 'He'd need room to haul them all in.'

'Those lobsters look savage,' said Dekko. 'I wouldn't fancy it if one of them got out and attacked.' He made snapping pincer movements at Orla with his hands.

'A lobster would have no chance against *me*,' said Orla. 'I'd hook it on the end of my line, just like that!' She flung her rod back as if landing a huge fish.

'Do you think we really could catch a fish, I mean actually out of the sea?' asked Dekko.

'Well, that's where they *are*, all right,' Orla smiled, 'and I've caught fish before, in rivers.'

'Let's give it a go,' said Dekko. 'There's no one around. We'll borrow the boat and take it out.'

Orla couldn't help being impressed by the way he seized the chance of an adventure.

'You're on!' she said. 'All aboard!'

They went down the stone steps to where the boat was moored and pulled the rope so that the boat came up to them. Then they untied the rope and stepped in, sitting down side by side and taking an oar each. The only people on the quayside were holiday visitors, who probably thought they were local kids going out for a trip.

Beyond the harbour entrance they felt the boat rocking on the swell of the sea. It was a lot rougher than any rowing they had done before on rivers or lakes, but they were soon pulling the oars in time together and heading out to sea the way Joe had gone. Then they felt the current carrying the boat towards the island. There was no chance to fish, for they had to keep hold of their oars to control the boat. They came in at the little beach. Dekko jumped out and grabbed the rope. They pulled the boat up and away from the water.

'I don't know why Joe went on so much about the currents,' said Dekko. 'That was easy enough.'

'We followed his route,' said Orla, 'and luckily the sea was calm too.'

'Let's hope that means there'll be plenty of fish lolling about in it.' Dekko smiled.

Orla tried casting her line into the water from the shore, but she caught nothing.

After a while Dekko tried, but he too caught nothing. 'This is boring,' he said. 'Come on, let's explore.'

Orla took the rod and flicked the line back out of the water. It went flying behind her, and the hook caught on something. She found it was snagged on a tree root that was sticking out from the rocky bank of earth where the little beach ended. She went to untangle it.

'Look,' she said. 'There's a sort of hollow in the earth behind the root, like a little tunnel. I can reach my hand in.' As she did so, they seemed to hear a faint howling in the wind, a cry like a lonely voice. They looked at one another.

'Just the wind,' said Dekko. 'Be careful reaching into that hole, there might be a snake hiding in there.'

'Saint Patrick chased *them* all out of Ireland ages ago,' said Orla. 'Don't they teach you anything at your school?'

'Yes, they teach us that some girls think they're know-alls,' said Dekko, laughing.

Orla grinned. 'Well, I know *this*,' she said. 'I've found something in this hidey-hole. It feels like metal.'

Again, a bleak voice seemed to sound in the wind. Dekko was too excited to take any notice. 'Treasure,' he cried. 'Let's dig!'

'It's only small,' said Orla. 'I think I can pull it out.' Slowly, she brought her arm out of the hole. She held up her earth-smeared hand. She was holding what looked like a small chunk of metal. 'What can it be?' she wondered.

Dekko took it from her. 'I know what it looks like,' he said. 'A boat! Like a model, or a toy boat.' He began to rub the object. When the dirt came off they could see it was like brass, and had the shape of a boat with sails.

'It looks like a model of one of the Armada ships,' said Orla with wonder. 'I've seen pictures of them.'

'Hey, maybe it's gold!' said Dekko. 'Who could have hidden it here?'

They looked at one another. 'Do you think it belonged to—?' Orla didn't finish the sentence.

'The cabin-boy,' exclaimed Dekko. 'That could be it. It must have been a kind of mascot or something.'

'Maybe it was the only valuable thing he had,' said Orla. 'So he hid it away, to dig out later.'

'Let's take it – it could make us rich!' Dekko cried.

'If it *is* his,' said Orla quietly, 'I think we should leave it. Taking it would be like digging up a grave.'

'You mean he'd come and haunt us?' Dekko smiled. He made a high, spooky sound: 'Woo-eeeeeeeeee!' Then they both stopped very still. There seemed to be an answering sound, like the faint cry in the wind which they had heard before. They looked at one another again.

'The wind, it must have been the wind,' said Dekko hastily.

They looked at the trees and saw the leaves waving and rustling. Out at sea, the white tops of the waves were curling and flinging up spray.

'Yes, the wind,' said Orla, trying to sound sure of herself. 'We'd better go back.' She held up the little boat and looked enquiringly at Dekko as she moved towards the hole in the bank.

'OK, we'll put it back,' he said. Orla thrust her hand into the hole and brought it out. It was empty. She pushed some earth back into the hole to block it. Again, they seemed to hear the cry mingled with the wind, but now it sounded less forlorn.

They dragged the boat down the beach and jumped into it.

When they rowed out to sea they found the water was much rougher than it had been when they rowed in. The boat rocked about as they tried to guide it. The wind was getting stronger.

'How will we find the right way through the currents?' said Dekko.

The wind seemed to be almost shrieking now. They both heard a sound that mingled with it, like a child's voice, wailing: '*Derecha . . . Derecha . . .*'

Dekko shivered. 'What is it?' he stammered. 'Did you hear it?'

'I did,' said Orla. 'It sounded like *derecha*. It means *right* in Spanish. We must turn the boat to the right.'

'Can you believe it?' gasped Dekko. He was glad that Orla sounded so sure of herself.

'I don't know what to believe,' said Orla, 'but the sea's getting rougher by the minute. It could be our only hope.'

'What if he's trying to lure us on to the rocks?' asked Dekko. 'You heard what Joe said about him.'

'We don't have any choice, Dekko,' said Orla quietly. 'We'll have to trust him.' They rowed and rowed to the right. They seemed to be moving parallel to the harbour shore, but not towards it.

Then the wind shrieked again, and again they seemed to hear a word mingled with it. This time it was '*Izquierda . . . Izquierda . . .*'

'That's the word for *left*,' said Orla.

'Let's row for it,' said Dekko. 'A crew's got to stick together.'

'All for one and one for all,' shouted Orla.

They changed the boat's direction. Now, as the waves buffeted against them and the spray hit their faces, they did seem to be getting nearer to the harbour. On and on they rowed, with all the energy they could manage, panting and gasping as they pulled on the oars. They turned their heads and could see people standing on the rocky strand that ran along near the harbour. As they got closer, they could make out Orla's father and Dekko's mother among them, waving and shouting. Joe O'Brien was beside them.

They were almost at the shore now. Joe O'Brien waded out and grabbed the bow of the boat. He took the rope and pulled as Orla and Dekko gave a final drag at the oars and felt the boat ground itself on the pebbles. They were helped out and stumbled up the slope, where they each collapsed on to a rock, and sat gasping for breath.

In a jumble they could hear the words of relief and comfort as well as those of anger and accusation. Joe O'Brien said, 'You're a pair of bold kids, but thank God you're safe. I saw you from my lobster boat but it was too rough to get close to you. I came back here to raise the alarm. We were going to bring out the lifeboat. I don't know how you found your way back through those waters without help.'

'Maybe we did have help,' said Orla softly, smiling at Dekko. Together they walked down the strand to the water's edge. Orla gave a wave at the churning sea and called out, '*Muchas gracias*!'

Dekko waved too, and shouted, '*Muchas gracias*! . . . and *Olé*!'

STONE-AGE PEIG

Herbie Brennan

Stone-Age Peig was out hunting in Leinster on the morning of her tenth birthday when she found a baby wolf cub.

The little fellow was skin and bone as if he hadn't eaten in a while, which was probably the truth of it since his back leg was caught between two rocks and he couldn't get it out. His eyes had a bluish tinge you only see in cubs and he looked very, very weak.

All the same, he growled at Stone-Age Peig when she approached, showing tiny little needle teeth.

'What a fierce boy you are!' Peig said, grinning. 'Have you got yourself stuck? Have you got yourself stuck, little wolfie?' She ran her hand along his silky back.

The cub stopped growling and eyed her suspiciously as she bent over to examine his trapped leg. It didn't look injured, but it was stuck tight.

Stone-Age Peig pushed the haft of her spear between the two rocks. Little Wolfie whimpered softly but she ignored him. She pulled on the spear and invented the lever. The rocks parted at once.

Little Wolfie jerked his leg free with a look of surprise.

'Off you go, Little Wolfie!' cried Stone-Age Peig, expecting him to run away.

But Little Wolfie didn't run away. Little Wolfie wriggled forward on his stomach and licked her hand.

'Shoo!' said Stone-Age Peig, waving her arms about.

The wolf cub stopped and looked at her with interest but trotted after her again as soon as she moved off.

'Shoo!' said Stone-Age Peig again. 'Go back to your mother!' Now she thought about it, she wondered where Little Wolfie's mother might be. Grown-up wolves ate people.

Peig stopped again and looked around for Little Wolfie's huge, fierce mother. Little Wolfie sat down and watched her.

After a while, Stone-Age Peig decided that none of Little Wolfie's relatives were nearby. She sighed with relief and started off again. Little Wolfie followed.

He was still following when she got home.

Stone-Age Peig lived with her Stone-Age tribe in a warren of caves that riddled a cliff face overlooking the spot where Dublin would be built when the Vikings arrived.

But that wasn't due to happen for several thousand years. Just now there was the bay and the river and the five great tracks the people used and nothing much else except the surrounding forest.

Stone-Age Peig's elder sister, Stone-Age Brenda, was washing out a loincloth in the river when Peig trotted up.

'Is that all you brought back for supper?' Brenda asked sourly.

Peig stared at her with saucer eyes. 'That's not for supper!' she said, shocked. 'That's Little Wolfie – he's my *friend*!'

Just then their mother, Stone-Age Mrs Morrissy, walked out of their cave. 'You can't make friends with a *wolf*, Peig,' she said kindly. 'He'd eat us all when he grew up. Your sister's quite right: best we have him for our supper – I can add him to the stew I'm stewing.'

With that she swooped on Little Wolfie and carried him into the cave.

Peig heard him howl in terror, then there was a splash and silence.

Peig ran.

She tripped on several rocks because of the tears that blurred her eyes, but she kept on running until she reached the forest edge.

Then she stopped.

123

All the children of the tribe were warned they should never go into the forest, which was full of bears, hares, sabre-toothed cats, poisonous rats, warthogs, wild dogs and even snakes – since this was long before St Patrick banished them from Ireland.

'You must never, never take so much as a single step into the deep, dark, dreadful forest,' Peig's mother had once told her.

'Blow that for a game of Stone-Age soldiers!' Peig exclaimed aloud. She hated her sister Brenda. She hated her mother Mrs Morrissy.

She sniffed disdainfully and stepped into the deep, dark, dreadful forest.

She was sorry straight away. The forest was cold and dense and full of creepy sounds. Leaves shook and branches rustled. Things she couldn't see slunk through the undergrowth. Something grunted nearby. In distant depths things growled and howled.

Peig knew she should turn right round and walk back out of the forest, but she didn't do it because she couldn't do it, not after what her mother and her sister had just done to Little Wolfie.

So Peig strode deeper into the dark forest, following a track made by an animal with paws and claws. 'I'll never eat a stew made out of Little Wolfie,' she told herself. 'I'll never go back home again. I'll live all by myself and be the world's first vegetarian.'

And as an afterthought she muttered, 'If something eats me, it will serve them right.' By *them* she meant her mother and her sister.

She followed the track through undergrowth and squelchy bog until she reached a clearing by a stream.

She crouched to take a drink when something with a sleek, black pelt and strong, white teeth crept up behind her.

It was Stone-Age Father O'Shaughnessy, the tribal shaman. He was wearing his official panther pelt and great white shark's teeth collar.

'Hello, Father,' Peig said, scuffing at the ground with one bare foot. The look he gave her had her feeling guilty already.

'What are you doing in the forest, child?' asked Stone-Age Father O'Shaughnessy grimly.

'Nothing, Father,' Peig said, avoiding his eye. *What was Father O'Shaughnessy doing in the forest*? Peig thought crossly, but she was afraid to ask.

'Why aren't you home in your cave looking after your poor old mother?'

'I don't know, Father,' Peig said.

'You don't know?' asked Stone-Age Father O'Shaughnessy. 'You don't *know*? Do you know that—'

A large brown bear lumbered out of the forest into the clearing.

'B-b-b—' Peig stammered, eyes wide, pointing.

'Don't interrupt me, child,' snapped Stone-Age Father O'Shaughnessy. 'Do you know that it is a child's duty – *your* duty – to—'

But Peig never found out what it was her duty to do. The large brown bear caught up Stone-Age Father O'Shaughnessy in a large brown bear hug.

Although Peig didn't much like Stone-Age Father O'Shaughnessy, she couldn't very well let him be eaten.

'Stop that!' she shouted. But the bear ignored her.

Stone-Age Father O'Shaughnessy turned pink. 'Ugh,' he said. 'Ugh, ugh.'

Peig took her spear and poked the bear in his shoulder. The bear ignored her.

Stone-Age Father O'Shaughnessy turned red. 'Ow,' he said. 'Ow, ow.'

Peig poked the bear in his back. The bear ignored her.

Stone-Age Father O'Shaughnessy turned blue. 'Ohhhh,' he said. 'Ohhhh, ohhhh.'

Peig poked the bear in his bear bottom. The bear dropped Stone-Age Father O'Shaughnessy and launched himself at Peig with a roar that shook the treetops.

Peig dropped her spear and ran.

She ran twice around the clearing and the bear ran after her.

She ran right across the stream and the bear ran after her.

She ran left and right and right and left and up and down and round and round and still the bear ran after her.

Eventually, she ran back into the deep, dark, dreadful forest.

She could hear the bear crashing through the undergrowth behind her as she hurled herself forward desperately.

The bear was very, very close behind her when she found herself beside a rocky, earthen bank. It was too high to climb, but there was a little cave-mouth no more than a few feet away. Peig reckoned it was just large enough for her to squeeze inside, but not large enough for the bear to follow.

Peig hurled herself into the opening and wriggled down a narrow passage to get away from the bear. The passage opened up into a den. Inside the den was a sabre-toothed cave lion.

'Grrr!' said the sabre-toothed cave lion.

'Yipes!' said Stone-Age Peig.

Peig popped from the cave-mouth like a cork from a bottle, although there were no corks in Ireland in those days and no bottles to put them in either.

Fortunately the bear had wandered off a little way otherwise she might well have been trapped. But she had no time to thank her Stone-Age stars since the sabre-toothed cave lion was so close behind her, she could feel his breath on her legs.

Peig raced past the bear and shinned up the nearest tree. She perched on a bough and looked down. Below her, the cave lion had begun to climb the tree.

Peig gulped and climbed higher.

Below her the bear began to climb the tree after the cave lion.

Peig gulped again and climbed higher still. With so many things climbing it, the tree began to sway.

It was swaying quite a lot by the time Peig reached the top.

Clinging to the treetop, Peig looked down. Below her and quite close now, the cave lion was still climbing the tree. Below him and not much further away, the bear was still climbing the tree.

'At least things can't get any worse,' sighed Stone-Age Peig.

She was entirely wrong. A cloud of Stone-Age buzzy bees began to swarm around her head.

'Get away!' screamed Peig, who hated buzzy bees.

The cave lion was more than halfway up the tree now and still climbing steadily. The bear was only just behind.

'Get away!' screamed Peig again, waving her arms around so violently that she nearly fell right off her branch.

The cave lion was just yards away and licking his sabre-toothed lips. The bear was at his heels.

Peig's wildly waving arms struck the beehive of the buzzy bees, knocking it off the branch.

Time seemed to slow as she watched it tumble over and over on its way towards the ground, followed by the bees. But it never reached the ground. It struck the head of the sabre-toothed lion and burst wide-open, covering him in honey.

At once the bear seized the lion, trying to lick off the honey. They wrestled together, bear and lion, until they both fell off the tree.

Peig climbed down the other side and trotted back the way she'd come, to find out if Stone-Age Father O'Shaughnessy was all right after his big, brown bear hug.

'You saved my life!' cried Stone-Age Father O'Shaughnessy as she stepped into the clearing. 'You must let me do something for you!'

He looked as if he might be about to kiss her and Peig stepped back hurriedly. She wondered if he could put a curse on her rotten mother, but she only said, 'That's all right, Father – you don't have to do anything.'

'But there must be something you want!' screamed Stone-Age Father O'Shaughnessy excitedly. 'There must be something I can do for you!'

The only thing Peig wanted was her Little Wolfie back but it was too late for that now. The thought of bits of him bubbling in the stew brought tears streaming down her cheeks.

'What's the matter?' Stone-Age Father O'Shaughnessy asked kindly. He put one arm round her shoulder and Peig was so miserable she didn't even pull away. In a moment she had told him everything, from the time she found Little Wolfie to the sound of him dropping into her mother's stew.

'I suppose I could try a Stone-Age Resuscitation Dance,' said Stone-Age Father O'Shaughnessy thoughtfully.

Peig stopped sobbing and looked at him wide-eyed. 'You mean you can bring Little Wolfie back to life?' she asked.

Stone-Age Father O'Shaughnessy frowned. 'Depends whether your mother cut him up before she dropped him in the stew. If he's whole, there's still a chance.' He wrapped his panther skin round himself decisively. 'Let's go and find out! But we must hurry – there might not be much time!'

'Ah, is it yourself, Father?' exclaimed Peig's mother, Stone-Age Mrs Morrissy, as they ran up to her cave. 'Would you like a cup of tea?'

Stone-Age Father O'Shaughnessy shuddered violently since Stone-Age tea was made from nettles and snake venom in Stone-Age times. 'No thank you, Mrs Morrissy,' he said breathlessly. 'Where's the wolf cub Stone-age Peig brought back this morning?'

'Ah, the little divil is inside the cave,' said Mrs Morrissy. 'You'll be staying for a bite of dinner, won't you, Father? We're having tender young wolf st—'

But both Peig and the shaman were already running towards the cave.

Little Wolfie met them at the cave-mouth. He looked wet, but otherwise unharmed. He growled uncertainly at Stone-Age Father O'Shaughnessy, but wagged his tail delightedly when he saw Peig.

'Little Wolfie!' Stone-Age Peig cried. 'You're all right!'

'I'm only after giving him a bath, Father,' explained Stone-Age Mrs Morrissy as she hurried up to join them. 'To get rid of his fleas so.' She shrugged her shoulders to adjust her Irish elk skin. 'Nothing worse than fleas for ruining the flavour of a stew.'

'And what do you propose to do with him now?' asked Stone-Age Father O'Shaughnessy.

'Well, the mincer's broken so I thought I'd dice him. I'll save the bones for stock, of course.'

Stone-Age Father O'Shaughnessy fixed her with a gimlet eye, although no gimlets had yet been invented. 'You must never put a washed wolf in a beef stew,' he told her grimly. 'The Stone-Age Pope's just ruled it's fierce bad luck.'

'But what will I do with him at all, at all?' wailed Stone-Age Mrs Morrissy.

'You shall give him to your daughter Peig to look after,' said Stone-Age Father O'Shaughnessy firmly. 'And her elder sister Brenda can clean up if he makes a mess.' He turned to Peig and winked. 'That'll be right now, won't it, Stone-Age Peig?'

'Indeed it will!' said Stone-Age Peig.

DRIVING
TO ACHILL

David O'Doherty

'We'll never fit that into the car,' Mum would warn me, pointing at my overfilled going-away bag lying by the front door. 'What have you put in there?'

'Just a few important things,' I'd reply, doing my best to sound surprised.

'Such as?'

'Oh, some Lego, a couple of Star Wars men . . .'

'Come on, it weighs a ton.'

'A board-game too. A couple of board-games. My stamps . . .'

'Your stamps!' she'd laugh, like I'd said something funny. 'Are you really sure you need to bring your stamp collection away on summer holiday?'

'Well . . . no. I suppose not.'

'What else have you packed?'

'My football . . .'

'The big one or the small one?' Mum knew all of my stuff.

'Both.'

'Both?' she'd sigh wearily. 'But your old ball is down there already.'

'I'll need my skateboard . . .' I'd try to insist.

'But the roads on Achill are too bumpy for it.'

'Well, my jigsaws then, and all my books . . .'

'All of your books! We're only going for two weeks . . . and you haven't done a jigsaw in years. By the way, which clothes are you bringing?'

'Oh yes,' I'd mumble, 'clothes.' In the excitement of going away there was always something I forgot to pack.

'Pigeon,' she'd only ever call me Pigeon when she was running out of patience, 'maybe you should bring your bag back upstairs, take everything out and have another go.'

'OK.' There'd be no point in trying to argue. I wouldn't win. I'd haul it back to my room, while my perfect brother and sister, who were seven and eight years older than me and never got into trouble or did anything wrong, brought their perfectly-sized luggage out to the car.

'And hurry up,' my brother would call out. 'If you're not ready in ten minutes we're leaving without you!'

It was two hundred miles across the country from our grey Dublin street to Granny's cottage on Achill Island. The drive could take five to six hours, depending on whether or not we pulled in to eat our sandwiches and the number of pee-stops along the way. I knew the journey very well. We went there for a week every Easter and two weeks in the summer. It took a long time, but I didn't mind. Achill was, and still is, the most marvellous place I have ever been.

Achill isn't really an island – well, it is – but it has a bridge connecting it to the mainland. Granny's cottage was six miles from the bridge, near a tiny village called Dugort which, my father would tell us each time we passed through it, is the next Irish town after Dublin in alphabetical order. The cottage sat on the side of a hill by the sea. In front of it was a steep, green field and below that a beach that only we knew about. You couldn't see it from the road and it didn't appear on any of the tourist maps. It was our own secret beach, where we could swim and fish and build rafts and bonfires, and do thousands of other amazing things we couldn't do in the city.

Dad always insisted that we leave Dublin at ten o'clock, after morning rush-hour. We had to go through the city to get on to the N4, or whatever road Mum had chosen from the blue Esso roadmap in the glove box. The map was so old it didn't have any of the new roads on it. Dad said it was so old it was written in Viking, which we knew wasn't true, because the Vikings didn't speak Viking, or have Esso roadmaps.

The first ten miles driving through the suburbs took ages. Lots of stopping and starting, and sets of traffic lights to wait in line for as we passed rows and rows of houses just like ours. Everywhere people were going about their daily routines – walking the dog, cutting the grass, cycling to the shop – too busy to notice our red Renault car, packed full of swimming togs and wellies and fishing rods. It made me want to lean out the window and yell at the top of my lungs, 'EVERYBODY LOOK AT US, WE ARE GOING ON HOLIDAY!'

Out into County Kildare the houses were fewer, and further apart, separated by bright, green fields dotted with cows. 'See the white cows,' Dad would say in his best know-all voice.

'Yes,' we'd nod from the back.

'They're white because they're full of milk. And the black ones are black because they're empty. And the black and white ones are black and white because they're half full.'

And I would believe him until my brother and sister screamed, 'DAAAD, THAT'S RUBBISH,' and Mum would smile and shake her head.

'Calm down. I'm just joking,' Dad would laugh. 'Anyway, everyone knows the black and white ones are black and white because they are full of Guinness.'

Then we'd all scream together, 'DAAAD!'

Being the youngest of three was tough on long car journeys. I always had to sit in the middle of the back seat. Not only was this the least comfortable place in the car, but it also meant that:

(a) I didn't have my own window to open and close, or fog up with my breath to write mean things about the other members of the back seat.

and

(b) I was constantly open to the threat of a 'Human Sandwich' (also known as a 'Game of Squash').

A Human Sandwich always took place like this:

My sister: 'Hey I'm hungry.'

My brother: 'Me too.'

My sister: 'Do you know what I'd love?'

Both together: 'A HUMAN SANDWICH!'

And they would slide towards each other along the seat, crushing me until I complained to Mum and she threatened to make us walk the rest of the way.

Across the flat middle of the country we would go, passing through towns with exotic-sounding names like Roosky, Tulsk and Bohola. There were the usual things to look out for – the sailboat races on Lough Ennell near Mullingar; the roadworks at Kinnegad that had been in progress since before I was born; the sign in front of the Percy French Hotel in Strokestown that always had a few letters missing. One year it would be the PERC RENCH HOTE, next the ERCY FREN OTEL.

'Let's play the Car Game,' my brother would announce. 'I pick Toyota.'

The Car Game was where everyone chose a make of car, and for five minutes counted how many of those cars they saw passing by. The winner was the person who counted the most.

'I'll have Datsun,' my sister would say.

'Ford,' Mum would chip in.

'Renault,' Dad would pat the logo on the steering wheel.

Not having much interest in cars, I

wouldn't be able to think of any other makes.

'Rolls Royce,' my brother would whisper to me. 'Rolls Royce,' I'd say out loud, and never spot a single one, because there were only about five Rolls Royces in all of Ireland.

Tarmonbarry is close to halfway. It was where we stopped for lunch if, according to Dad's strict time schedule, we had time to stop. Like most midland towns Tarmonbarry has a few pubs, a church, and a couple of shops, but it has something else too. Something else that made it the most interesting place in the whole world to stop and eat your cheese sandwich. In the middle of Tarmonbarry is an enormous steel and concrete bridge, spanning the River Shannon, that can open like a castle drawbridge to let boats through. And the boats lined up waiting for it to open weren't ordinary boats. They were big, white Shannon cruisers with upstairs and downstairs cabins, and cockpits full of controls like spaceships. And I wouldn't be able to sit still any longer. I'd have to get out and run up and down the quayside, shooting at the human-looking space mutants that piloted the spaceship with my invisible laser gun.

*

Then we'd be off again, following the signs to Westport. Westport is the last big town before Achill Island. It has a train station and a small zoo which Mum always said we should visit next time. But we never did, because just past the sign for the zoo is another sign that would fill us with excitement and make us stamp our feet in anticipation: ACHILL 40 miles.

After Westport the scenery changed again. The roads became narrower as they wound around the great mountains of County Mayo. The colour of the landscape changed too, from bright green to yellowy brown. There weren't as many cows, but hundreds of sheep in every direction. Sometimes a flock would block the road in front of us and Dad would have to inch the car slowly through them, letting me lean over to beep the horn, while my brother and sister stared out their windows at the bobbing sea of live woolly jumpers.

After the ruined castle at Newport that once belonged to Grace O'Malley, the Pirate Queen of all Ireland, the road unexpectedly swept around to the right. In front was our first glimpse of the Atlantic

Ocean. Wild waves crashed for the millionth time against the jutting rocks and high sea-cliffs. *Now they are real waves*, I would think to myself. *Not like the feeble things that lap up against the power station in Dublin Bay.*

We were almost there. A countdown from ten as the car rumbled over the rough tarmac on the short bridge across to the island, and then a cheer. Just a few miles left to Granny's. Dad would be full of plans for the holiday. 'We must try fishing down there,' he'd say, pointing off in one direction. 'We must climb that mountain this year,' and we'd nod in agreement, silently wishing he'd drive faster.

Passing the sign for Dugort he'd explain once again that it was the next Irish village after Dublin in alphabetical order. Before there was time to tell him we knew that already, the car would have pulled up at Granny's bright white cottage. We'd hear her dogs woof and she'd come out to meet us. A quick hug and I'd fire my neatly re-packed bag into the back bedroom, then head straight down the hill towards the beach. Thinking about the perfect lawn of golden sand that lay ahead, untouched since

Easter, wondering what interesting things had been washed up, I'd start to run faster . . . and faster . . . until I was sprinting flat-out. I had no time to waste. There were so many holes to dig, rafts to build, fish to catch, swims to swim – and only two weeks to fit it all in.

IMMIGRANTS

Gerard Whelan

(for Frank Murphy)

They'd only stopped to admire the world really, but then Alan had a tiny nibble at Africa and was starting on America when Mrs Marley came in and caught them. Dad, who'd been pretending not to notice Alan's nibbles, suddenly turned a look of stern disapproval on his children. Mrs Marley made a kind of strangled sound.

'The poor world!' she said. 'Leave the poor world alone!'

The big round cake was a beautiful thing. Sally Ann thought it was far too good looking to eat. It was decorated with coloured icing to look exactly like the earth itself. Mrs Marley had pored over a school atlas for hours, getting the shapes of the continents just right.

'Well, we don't know for sure where these people are from,' she explained. 'But they'll surely know the shape of the world better than we do. We don't want them to think that we're ignorant. They might be insulted.'

This was true, Sally Ann's dad agreed. Insults were far too important to be wasted: if you were going to insult someone then you should only do it on purpose. This wasn't Mrs Marley's attitude, of course: she just didn't like offending people. She was a lovely woman. The time she'd spent getting the shapes right was typical of her: no detail, people said, was too small for Mrs Marley. She'd made cake-making into an art form.

'America looks tasty,' Alan said. 'Is that icing almond or plain?'

The attempt to distract Mrs Marley with detail didn't work. The old lady knew Alan's sweet tooth too well. She came over and scrutinized Florida. It seemed slightly smaller than it had been when it left her kitchen.

'You ate Miami,' she said accusingly to Alan, who denied the accusation with all the injured innocence of the born liar that he was.

'You know, Alan,' Dad said admiringly, 'you could make a fine politician some day.'

Knowing what his dad thought of politicians, Alan stared at him suspiciously. Dad, seeing the look, explained.

'Look at Seán Morgan,' he said. 'When we were in school together he'd give wrong answers to simple questions and everybody thought he was just a fool. But then he went into politics and we realized he simply wasn't *able* to tell the truth, no matter what.

A liar born and bred, like all belonging to him. And look how well he's done for himself!'

The committee to welcome the refugees had organized a big party in the Parochial Hall, and the world-cake was going to be the centrepiece of a great buffet welcoming the newcomers. No one was sure what the strangers ate, so there'd been some concern about exactly what food should be laid on.

'Cakes!' Mrs Marley had said immediately, as though the answer was perfectly obvious. 'Plenty of cakes! Sure, everyone likes a cake.'

'They do, Mrs Marley,' Sally Ann's dad said. 'But sometimes, you know, they like something else with it – just for a change, like.'

Cakes were Mrs Marley's answer to everything, Dad said crossly sometimes when the old lady's fixation with pastry got on his nerves. But Alan saw absolutely nothing wrong with that idea, and even Mum – who was fond of Mrs Marley – would defend her.

'Maybe cakes *are* the answer to everything,' Mum would say. 'Have you ever thought of that? It's no dafter than the answers that some people have.'

'Such as what?' Dad challenged her once when she said that.

Challenging Mum was always a mistake. She began ticking off some people's answers to everything, on her fingers.

'War,' she said. 'Murder. Jail. Hanging . . .'

But Dad, remembering suddenly who he was dealing with, waved a desperate hand to stop her.

'You're perfectly right,' he said. 'I'll take the cakes.'

'Me too,' Alan chipped in. 'A jam doughnut, please, and an éclair.'

Dad sighed. 'It's our own children that we teachers most often fail with,' he said. 'Did you know that?'

'I'd sort of guessed it by this stage,' Alan said.

In a way, the actual contents of the buffet didn't matter. The party itself was a symbol as much as anything else: the point was to fill the place with lots of what the locals felt were Good Things, and offer them to the unfortunate strangers who'd come among them. '*Look*,' was the intended message to the newcomers, '*This is nourishment for us. These are things we value, and we have made them for you and we are giving them to you in abundance, to welcome you to our country.*'

Still, it wouldn't do to offer the wrong things. Sally Ann's dad said there'd been great fun at the meeting held to decide what the Good Things at the party should actually be. Alcohol was ruled out immediately, and boiled pigs' feet. In fact, knowing nothing of the newcomers' tastes, the committee ended up by deciding to stick to the sort of thing that just about everybody liked – that's to say cakes and biscuits, just as Mrs Marley had said. There'd be other things too, of course – roast meats of various kinds, and vegetables for the vegetarians, and ice cream and chocolates, and tea and coffee and milk and lemonade and what have you. It had taken the committee over four hours to reach this decision, and even then a couple of the more dedicated members had wanted to talk further about the matter.

'Sure, if they won't eat it,' Sally Ann's dad told the others at that stage, 'we'll eat it ourselves. In fact I wish it was all here right now – all this talk about food has left me starving.'

Indeed, when he came home afterwards he was so hungry that Sally Ann's mum made chips for him, and used up the last of Alan's emergency supply of Chicken Squiggles to go along with them. But even Alan didn't mind, because it was in a good cause. Dad had never eaten Chicken Squiggles before and before tasting the first, he held it up on the end of his fork and eyed it suspiciously. Then he got the packet from the freezer and studied the list of ingredients.

'Good Lord,' he said, sounding awed. 'Isn't it amazing the rubbish that we feed our children?'

But he ate all the Squiggles Mum cooked, even so, and seemed a bit disappointed that there weren't more.

Not everyone, of course, welcomed the prospect of having the refugees among them. It wasn't a big town, but it was inhabited by humans, and wherever there are humans there'll be as many suspicious minds as welcoming committees. Some people turn out to the world and welcome new things; others turn in and don't like changes in the little world they know. There were various dark mutterings about the strangers. What right had they to come here and use up the town's resources – which weren't much to begin with in any case? Who knew what strange ways they had, or what dirt and diseases they might bring with them? Some said they just wanted to come and scrounge on the country. Some said they mainly consisted of people who'd been criminals in their own lands – people who'd been in trouble with the police, and who would bring a crimewave to the town. The basic complaints, as Sally Ann's dad said, all added up to the same thing: the newcomers were different.

'And how would they not be different?' he wanted to know. 'It's a whole new world they're coming to. What's so wonderful about us, anyway, that it's such a crime not to be like us?'

Sally Ann's father taught in the local secondary school, and he'd travelled a lot when he was young. He had no time for all the rumours and the carping about the refugees in his home town now. Mostly he dismissed the mutterings with jokes, but not always. In fact, it was one of the few subjects on which his children had ever seen him grow close to getting angry, and both of them, in their different ways, rather admired him for it.

'There isn't a thing being said about those poor unfortunates that wasn't said one time about the Irish themselves,' he'd say. 'No matter who ran this country, we exported our poor and our hungry to wherever would have them, and we abandoned them to whatever might happen to them there. Dirty, criminal Paddy, with his strange food and strange ways and his dirt and his diseases – you still heard those things in England and even in America in my day, you know. And now here we are with a few quid, and unfortunates ask us for just a little bit of the mercy that other places showed to our people, and there's some of us can do no better than start off with the same old miserable tripe that we used to have thrown at ourselves.'

Sally Ann felt a rush of pride when he talked like that. Even Alan – who felt it was very important at his age not to be impressed by anything at all (with the possible exception of a good cake) – had to admit, that their dad, in this mood, was *almost* impressive. Sally Ann guessed that by 'impressive', Alan just meant 'tough'. Alan was two years older than her, but she was beginning to suspect that boys were a tiny bit slow in developing – though maybe that was just Alan.

'Is the brain the last bit to develop in the human male?' she asked her mum.

'I'm not sure,' Mum said. 'I'll wait for your father's to develop, and when it does I'll tell you.'

'Thanks, Mum,' Sally Ann said. Mothers were handy sometimes.

Dad didn't just vent his feelings about the anti-refugee lot in private. Whenever he heard someone make bad comments about the refugees he spoke out to them about it, and he could get quite angry with them too – angrier than he'd ever let his children see him. Once, Sally Ann had heard, he'd almost got in a fight with Matt Martin, the garage owner, in the lounge bar of the Horseshoe Hotel. Matt had set himself up as a sort of spokesman for the anti-refugee crowd, thinking it might be useful to him. But Matt Martin was a sly one, and far too canny to come to blows with anyone as big as himself; and Sally Ann's dad was a well-built man, so Matt had backed down. When Sally Ann heard about it she'd almost burst with pride. Like most sensible people she didn't like Matt Martin at all. Even his best friends, people said, didn't like Matt. There was something oily and secretive about him. The story had really impressed Alan, too: for some reason it was one of his main ambitions in life to see someone puck Matt Martin in the jaw.

The whole refugee question had put the local politician, Seán Morgan, in a bit of a fix. The political party he belonged to formed the government which had decided that the newcomers should settle in the town. The government hadn't really wanted to have to make this decision, but this was a special case: the Americans had taken a great interest in the matter, and so the Irish authorities had decided to settle the newcomers here. Why this little town in particular had been picked, nobody knew. Shortly after the news was announced, the government declared that a big American company was going to set up a research facility in the town, and that it would provide more jobs for the area than the place had ever had in its entire history. If the government had hoped that this piece of news would cheer up the complainers, it was disappointed.

'It's pure bribery!' Matt Martin said privately to Seán Morgan. 'Not that I've anything against bribery, of course, but it will probably never happen.'

But as the day of the refugees' arrival neared, it did seem that *something* was going to happen. Lots of well-dressed strangers started turning up, and public meetings were organized in the Parochial Hall to educate the locals in how they ought to react to the newcomers who'd soon be among them. When the first of these meetings was announced, Matt Martin was very scathing about it in the bar of the Horseshoe Hotel.

'They want to *educate* us!' he said. 'They want to send some young whippersnappers down from the city to *educate* us! Well, I'll tell you one thing – they won't educate Matt Martin!'

'He never spoke a truer word,' Sally Ann's mum said when he heard about that. 'An army of professors couldn't get an education into that man's mind with a crowbar.'

The public meetings were strange affairs. They were well attended from the first, especially by old ladies – the bingo hall had burned down the month before, and they were glad to have somewhere to socialize on the long summer evenings. The educators were all young men in suits who never stopped smiling and talked a lot of obvious nonsense, but the old ladies didn't mind. They were well used to having nonsense talked at them by various people, and most of them admired the way that the well-dressed young men looked.

'I never saw such clean people,' Mrs Marley said. 'You could eat your dinner off their shoes.'

'If you were that way inclined,' said Sally Ann's dad. He didn't especially like the educational sessions because he said that, as someone who talked nonsense all day for a living, the last thing he needed was to come and listen to it of an evening. After a few of the sessions, indeed, just about everyone was fed up with them. It was obvious that the young men knew no more than anyone else about the newcomers, and were just talking high-falutin' gibberish. Only old Mrs Coombes, who was ninety-six, seemed unperturbed by the gibberish, probably because she was as deaf as a post. But even Mrs Coombes found the perpetual smiles of these young men disturbing.

'No one can be that happy unless they're up to no good,' she'd say very loudly to Mrs Marley, her next door neighbour. 'It's not natural!'

'Not here, maybe, Mary Ellen,' Mrs Marley would say. 'But maybe it's natural in the city.'

To which Mrs Coombes would reply, as she replied to everything that everyone ever said to her, 'What did you say? Speak up! I'm stone deaf, you know.'

'How would I not know, Mary Ellen?' Mrs Marley asked patiently. 'You've been telling me at least ten times a day for the past twenty-five years.'

This was perfectly true, though there were still people who didn't know abut Mrs Coombes's little disability: she only wore her false teeth on special occasions, and was hard to understand without them.

'What did you say?' Mrs Coombes said

now. 'Speak up!'

Still, for better or worse, the great day had finally come, and it seemed as though the whole town had assembled in the square to see the refugees arrive. In the Parochial Hall long trestle tables almost sagged under heaped platters of food and great urns of drinks, and Mrs Marley supervised the ladies of the local branch of the Housewives Association as they fiddled with increasingly smaller details. Dad left to meet Mum and find a good spot in the crowd that was already gathering outside in the square. Sally Ann and Alan watched now as Mrs Marley took up the world-cake and, bearing it proudly, brought it out and put it in a place of honour on the main table. Alan looked around greedily at all the food, but Sally Ann stuck her elbow in his ribs.

'Stop that!' she said. 'You're dribbling. You'll get nothing here – those old ones have eyes like hawks.'

Alan looked at an enormous brown lump of *something* that dominated one of the side-tables.

'What in the name of God is *that* supposed to be?' he asked.

'I think,' Sally Ann said, 'that it used to be some class of a cow. In a former life, like.'

Alan was awed by the sheer *number* of

edibles in the Hall. Mrs Marley and her minions had outdone themselves. But eventually, even Alan had to admit that Sally Ann was right about the hawk-eyed women: not even a fly was going to get near the food before the appointed hour. They wandered outside to see if anything was stirring. There was a buzz of hushed talk from the crowd, which had grown enormously since they went into the Hall. A platform had been set up at one end of the square, and on it Seán Morgan sat in state on a red plastic chair while members of the local Council bickered about who'd sit where on the chairs that were left. A few seats were reserved for some senior Americans, but they hadn't yet arrived. None of the well-dressed young men with clean shoes was to be seen at all. Some security types, though, were out in force, mingling with the crowd and making a useless attempt, with their dark suits and their shared air of snake-like menace, to fit in with the locals.

A long, black limousine drove into the square, stilling the hum of expectation. It drew up in front of the platform and three men in suits got out. The crowd started murmuring again when one was recognized as the leader of the government and another as the Minister for Defence. The third man was elderly and looked far too dignified to be a politician. Someone recognized him and an eager whisper ran round the crowd that this was the US Ambassador to Ireland. The three men mounted the steps to the platform where Seán Morgan, looking flummoxed in the presence of someone genuinely important, quickly yielded his central seat.

By this stage Sally Ann had seen her dad and mum in the front of the crowd and she went over to them. Alan had gone to find his mates.

'Is that really the American ambassador?' Sally Ann asked her dad.

'Seemingly so,' he said.

'Where's your troublesome brother?' Mum asked.

'Making trouble somewhere with his troublesome friends,' Sally Ann said.

More black cars came, bringing more dignitaries. Sally Ann saw Matt Martin in the crowd, eating an ice cream. Now that the great day was actually here, he looked as excited as anyone else. The local silver band turned up, their instruments gleaming, and marched to a spot directly in front of the platform, where by now the distinct short-age of chairs was causing scuffles among some of the councillors. Sally Ann looked at her watch. It was five to twelve – five minutes before the newcomers were due.

'They must be important all the same,' her mum said.

'True,' her dad said. 'You don't get such bigwigs turning out for just anybody.'

The day was dry, but the sky was cloudy. Some of the clouds seemed to gather directly overhead, as though they too wanted to see the newcomers arrive. As the minutes ticked away, the crowd fell silent, even the little children. The tension mounted and at two minutes to twelve Sally Ann felt suddenly breathless and discovered that she'd actually forgotten to breathe. She looked up at her dad. He smiled down at her but his face was tight with expectation. He put an arm round her shoulders. Alan appeared, without a cheeky grin on his face, so that it took Sally Ann a few moments to recognize him.

'I thought we should all be together for it,' he said. He stood beside Dad, who put his free hand on his son's shoulder. Mum too touched her children. A tingle ran down Sally Ann's spine. The very air felt electric. Then she looked at Alan and to her astonishment saw that his hair was beginning to lift, to stand away from his head. She felt her own hair start to do the same. When she looked around she saw that the same thing was happening to everyone whose hair was in any way long.

'Dad?' she said, a little frightened. 'Mum?'

'Static,' Dad said soothingly. There was an air of wonder in his voice. 'They warned us about that on the news, remember? It's caused by the electrical field.'

Suddenly Sally Ann did remember hearing about the effect, and she giggled: it looked weird to see all of these people with their hair standing on end, even Mrs Brady, the doctor's wife, who was always so pompous. You wouldn't have thought that anything, even electricity, would dare to interfere with her. But Mrs Brady didn't seem to notice her own floating hair. She was staring up at the sky, and she didn't look pompous now at all: she looked awestruck. Sally Ann's eyes followed Mrs Brady's gaze upwards, and then she forgot about the doctor's wife completely. Above the square something big and white was poking through the low grey clouds. Sally Ann stared – everyone in the crowd stared, even the bigwigs on the platform. The white thing was the edge of a vast, silver-coloured disk. Strings of neon blue, white and violet electricity flared and died like baby lightning flashes across its surface. As it descended through the cloud, more and more of it became visible.

'Oh, my,' Sally Ann heard her mother murmur from behind her. 'Oh, my, oh, my.'

The craft was through the cloud now, hovering maybe fifty metres overhead. It was bigger than the whole square and cut off most of the sunlight. Still the people underneath watched in silence, overwhelmed. The craft too was totally silent, except for the little crackle from the electricity flowing over its silver skin. Gradually, even this died away. Sally Ann had no idea how long that took, but exactly as the last, twisting, neon worm of power died on the white hull above, a great column of milky light came from the base of the ship and hit the square. It stood there, opaque as a marble column, and then Sally Ann saw that something was moving inside it. And then the thing that was moving inside it moved out, and stood in the middle of the square watched by hundreds of wide, wide eyes. And the column of milky light disappeared, leaving the something just standing there, facing its new hosts.

It was more than three metres high, and it was shaped like the haystacks Sally Ann had seen in her grandparents' photograph albums. Thick arms like tentacles drooped from the haystack, and stubby little legs as wide as the trunks of big trees supported it. From the top of the haystack grew a long, thick, snake-like thing that had to be a neck, supporting a head shaped like a very large football. The creature was coloured a sort of avocado green. Its metre-long neck coiled around, gracefully but uncertainly, and two yellow eyes, the size and shape of tennis balls, looked unblinkingly round the square. Still, there was no sound. All the creatures in the square stood silently, looking at each other. Dignitaries on the platform seemed almost to be cowering. None made a move to approach what was obviously the refugee spokesman. For a moment no one even stirred. Then, in the deep, deep silence, Sally Ann heard footsteps, and a figure emerged form the crowd. It was Mrs Marley. The old woman walked into the middle of the square and looked around. Then, when she saw how still everyone was, she looked up at the creature and smiled. Mrs Marley was carrying a big platter, piled high with scones and rock buns. She walked over until she stood right in front of the stranger and looked up at it, so small herself that she had to crane her neck to make eye contact.

'You must think we're awfully rude,' Mrs Marley said. 'Would you like one of my scones? They're buttered already.'

One of the great tentacles coiled up, and its tapering tip hovered delicately over the

167

plate Mrs Marley held up for inspection. Then it raised a golden brown scone to its lipless mouth and, showing a great many sharp teeth, nibbled at it gracefully.

'My word!' the creature said 'What a beautiful scone!'

Its voice was flutingly musical.

'Light as air!' it said. 'Is it your own recipe?'

'My mother's,' Mrs Marley said proudly, trying hard not to show her pleasure at this conquest of a new world.

'I shall have to get it from you,' the creature said. 'My own scones always come out rock-hard. They never rise, you see.'

'Sounds to me like you need more baking soda,' Mrs Marley said.

The creature took another nibble, and looked again around the square.

'I'm supposed to meet some people here,' it said. 'We were told to come. We're refugees, you know. Our planet had an accident.'

'Oh, indeed,' Mrs Marley said, 'sure, I know all about you.' Which was an exaggeration, of course – though perhaps not: certainly Mrs Marley had just found out all that *she* needed to know about the newcomers.

Mrs Marley nodded towards the still-dubious politicians on the platform.

'I suppose them fellows in the suits are the ones you've to meet,' she said. 'But when your business is done, you bring your people into the hall there. There's lashings of good things for everyone, and we can all get to know one another a bit. You're all very welcome to Ireland, I'm sure, and I'll talk to you later. Do you want to take another scone, in case the speechifying goes on a bit? You must be hungry after your journey.'

'I am a little peckish,' the creature admitted. 'I think I'll try a rock bun this time, if I may. They look beautiful.' Its spare tentacle picked up a rock bun. 'We shall certainly talk later, ma'am,' the creature said. 'I'll look forward to it.'

Mrs Marley nodded and turned away with her plate. The creature, nibbling each of the little cakes in turn, began to walk towards the platform, where the politicians were regaining a bit of their self-control. The crowd seemed to release its collective breath. Sally Ann felt her face split in an enormous stupid grin, and when she looked around she saw that everyone else wore one too, even Matt Martin. When she looked up at her mum and dad they were smiling as well and looking at each other. Alan was staring after the creature.

'Bet he'd be good at wrestling,' he said. It was a compliment.

The crowd began to make noise again as people started to chatter excitedly. They seemed almost to have forgotten the great craft hovering silently overhead. Mrs Marley, smiling to herself, carried her platter of scones and rock buns back towards the Parochial Hall. The plate grew lighter with every step, as children and adults helped themselves to its contents. Mrs Marley didn't mind at this stage: it was time to start eating. Someone bumped into her roughly, and she almost dropped the platter. She clicked her lips impatiently.

'Really,' she said, thinking it was a child made careless by its desperate need for a rock bun. 'Manners, please.'

But when she turned it was only Mrs Coombes, who'd put in her false teeth for the occasion.

'Well, there's a big day for the town, Mary Ellen,' Mrs Marley said.

Mrs Coombes put her hand to her ear. 'Eh?' she said. 'What did you say? I'm stone deaf, you know.'

Mrs Marley smiled.

THE
BOATHOUSE

Michael Tubridy

The three of us went whizzing down towards the lake on our bikes. I was scared, excited, nearly dizzy with the bumps and speed and the sun flashing through the trees like disco lights. Jake was first because he has a snazzy bike. Gav was next because his bike isn't as banjaxed as mine.

We were on the last, steep stretch and my heart was pumping. Over a bump and my feet lost the pedals. I thought I was heading for the ditch. But then around the corner on to the flat, out of the trees, the lake dazzling me. My feet found the pedals, I braked hard and pulled up beside the other two.

Jake was laughing. 'Last time I came down there was with Donkey Brady. He got a puncture and went head first. Nearly took the kneecap off himself.'

Gav and me laughed too. Donkey's this galoot in our class, always breaking bones and getting caught.

'So where's the obstacle course yis made?' Jake asked, spitting one of his drippy little spits. Jake would never normally hang around with us but we'd met him in the Square just before we turned into the castle grounds. His two mates, Ross and Karl, were sick, so he'd tag along with us, he said. It's best not to say no to Jake.

'It's away on down past the boathouse,' Gav said.

'Ooh! Naughty, naughty! Down where little children shouldn't play,' Jake slagged.

'It's in the trees. No one will see it,' I said.

'Hey, who's them fishing?' Jake asked, pointing at two boys by the lake about half a football pitch away. Our town is so small, we were sure to know them. We pedalled in their direction.

'It's Francis and his little brother,' Gav said.

'Francis Saliva! Ith Fwanthith!' Jake spluttered, the way Francis does.

We pedalled slowly towards them, me last. Francis lives down the street from me and I didn't want his ma complaining to my ma the way she did when I threw my skateboard at him.

'Don't spray too much saliva in there, Fwanthith, or you'll fwighten the fith!' Jake called.

'Very funny, Mulligan! Now geth loth!' Francis called back.

Jake chucked his bike on the ground. 'I don't want to geth loth,' he said. 'I want to help you catch fith.' He picked up a rock the size of a Coke can and lobbed it into the lake near the end of Francis's line.

'Geth loth, Mulligan!' Francis yelped. 'You'll meth up my line!'

'I'm helping you, Francis. You need to stun the fish, make 'em all rise to the surface.' He lobbed in a bigger rock, exploding the water. 'Poachers use dynamite and the fish all rise to the surface. Easy! None of this standing around with a pound-shop rod.'

Francis looked like a fish that had just been landed, gasping for air, not sure how to cope. His brother tugged his sleeve. 'Come on, Francis,' he said, 'we'll head off.' He looked smarter than his big brother.

'Oh, stay where yis are!' Jake said, picking up his bike. 'We're off. See yis, saps. I mean thapth.'

He'd won. There was no need to stay. There was no real fun in frightening Francis.

We pedalled off along the track which skirts the lake, zigzagging around the potholes.

'Car tracks,' Gav said. 'Someone fishing probably.'

Jake pointed at the lake. 'Yeah, boat out there, near the island. One guy in it.'

'Could be Costigan,' I said. 'He sometimes goes out after school.'

Mr Costigan's our class teacher in fifth class. Jake hates him.

'Did you know Fwanthith back there's related to Costigan? Second cousin or something. Branner told me,' Jake said.

'Sure everyone's related to someone in this town,' Gav said. 'I'd hate to tell you some of the people I'm related to.'

'I'm not related to anyone in this town, thank God! I'd shoot myself if I was,' Jake said. He spat another of his drippy little spits. He does about nineteen a minute.

Jake came to live in Carrick two years ago, from Dublin. His mother moved here to live with Hughie Coyne who has the pub in Main Street. I heard my parents talking about them in their 'we're sensible, they're not' voices.

We were pedalling really slowly now, trying to nudge each other into the potholes. Jake's new Nike runners were muddy already and there were splashes on his Nike tracksuit. *Can you buy a Nike bike to match your outfit?* I thought of asking him, but I didn't. Jake's better at making jokes than at taking them. He'd no mudguards. Mudguards are for saps, he says.

'Costigan's a loser, same as Francis,' Jake said. 'All nerdy and thinks he's great.'

'He's better than Mrs Henchy last year,'

Gav said. 'She was soooooo boring.'

'What you think, Stevie?' Jake asked, nudging his front wheel into mine and pushing me into a puddle.

I'd have preferred if he hadn't asked. I like Costigan. So does Gav. And I'd have preferred if he hadn't called me Stevie. No one else does. Stephen's best. Steve's OK. I hate Stevie.

'Henchy's a wagon,' I said.

'What about Costigan? You're a Costigan kid, aren't you, Stevie?'

'No I'm not!' I said. 'Costigan's a pain! But at least he does art and PE with us, not like oul Wenchy knickers last year.'

Jake tried to mimic Costigan. 'Oboys-oboysoboys! I've eyes in the back of my head so none of your actin' the maggot! Are ye listenin' to me at all, at all?'

Gav and me half laughed. If he'd had his cronies with him, they'd have cracked up.

Jake put on a spurt. 'Come on! Where's this obstacle course? I want to see what youse saps get up to.'

A minute later we couldn't see the lake at all because of a screen of whispery reeds. This stretch of lakeshore was really squishy and my parents had warned me never to come down here. 'Too dangerous for kids messing about,' they'd said but that didn't stop me and Gav. We'd often chuck stones into the squish to see if they would sink. Today, though, we kept going until the boathouse came into sight.

'Hey, that's Costigan's car!' Gav said. It was parked right outside the boathouse and it was empty. We stopped beside it.

'Windows open too,' Jake said. 'Didn't expect us to be snooping around. Maybe we should let the air out of the tyres.'

'Boathouse is open too,' I said. 'I've never seen it open before.'

We stood at the door, peering in. It was like peering into a church, quiet and dark and echoey, except this church had water inside it and no end wall, so you could bring the boats in and out. There was just enough room for two long, narrow boats. One of them had gone and the other was rocking gently in the water.

'Yo!' Jake called and the boathouse called back, 'YOOOO!'

'It's like being in a cave looking out,' Gav said.

'Out!' I shouted.

'OOOUUUT!' the boathouse called back.

Jake nipped down the steps and hopped into the boat.

'Row, row, row the boat,' he chanted, jigging from one foot to the other, rocking the boat. 'Gently down the stream . . . all together now, boys!' He started jumping up and down like a mad thing and the boat was smashing against the wall of the boathouse and the echoes were going crazy. 'Merrily, merrily, merrily . . . oh, me butt!' He lost his balance and sat down hard. Gav and me were laughing the same nervy, hyper laugh. I needed to pee.

'That racket'll be all over the lake,' Gav said. 'Costigan'll hear it.'

'Costigan's thick!' Jake said, spitting a drippy spit. 'So thick he makes me sick. Hey, look!'

He'd hopped out of the boat and was back beside us. He was holding a coil of rope. 'Take this!' he grinned, handing it to Gav. 'You can use it in the obstacle course.' He bent down and picked up a padlock which was lying on the floor just inside the door.

'Costigan's a thick who makes me sick!' He waggled the padlock at us and grinned. 'What an interesting thought I've just had.'

'What?' I asked.

'What are padlocks for?'

'You wouldn't!' Gav said.

'Who wouldn't?'

'Wouldn't what?' I asked.

'Doh! Lock the door, stoopid!' Jake

sneered, waggling the padlock right in my face.

'I've got to have a pee,' I said, and dashed outside and behind a bush, even though there was no one else around.

When I came back, Jake had hooked the padlock through the bolt in the door. 'I now declare this boathouse locked!' he said, clicking it shut. 'Hee, hee! Very careless of Costigan, I must say.'

He stared hard at both of us. 'And no tales, OK? Else I'll have to say it was all Stevie's idea.'

Me and Gav looked at each other quickly.

'If my parents found out, there'd be murder, mystery and suspense,' I said.

'Same here,' Gav said.

'If my ma found out, she'd give me a tenner,' Jake said. 'She hates teachers.'

'Shhh!' I said. I'd heard a noise, an engine.

We all listened hard.

'Boat!' Gav said. 'Bet it's Costigan.'

We stared at each other, scared and thrilled.

'Let's split!' I said.

'Are you crazy?' Jake said. 'We have to see this. Come on. Hide!'

The engine was louder now though still quite far away.

'Into the trees,' Jake said. 'Take the bikes.'

There was no need to rush because we were completely screened by the thick mass of reeds, much taller than us, along the shore. Still, we hurried, pushing our bikes over rough ground, up a slope and into the trees, Gav with the coil of rope over his shoulder. We lay the bikes out of view, then threw ourselves on the ground in a row, just poking our heads up high enough to watch the action.

'What'll he do?' I asked.

'Strangle us,' Gav said.

'Don't be stupid,' I said. 'He can't know it was us.'

'Don't be so sure,' Jake said. 'We must've left fingerprints all over the kip. You weren't wearing gloves, were you?'

For a moment I felt panicky but then I realized he was messing.

'What will he do?' Gav asked.

'Into the boathouse,' Jake said. 'Curse when he finds the door locked. Hope we hear him!' he sniggered. 'Then he'll have to take the boat back out and come in through the reeds. Very messy.'

'The ground's really soft down there in the reeds,' Gav said. 'Maybe he'll sink when he gets out of the boat.'

'Up to his neck,' Jake said. 'And he'll scream and scream. Hee, hee, hee!'

We couldn't see the boat at all, but the sound of the engine told us it was near the boathouse. Then the sound died.

'Must be in it now,' Gav whispered.

'The eyes in the back of his head won't be much use to him now,' Jake cackled.

I wanted to clatter him for being so loud. Instead, I shut my eyes and counted to one hundred. When I opened them, nothing had happened.

After ten forevers the door of the boathouse rattled, then rattled again. I'd a sudden urge to run away but I didn't want to stand up. More rattles, then a pause, then muffled bumps and bangs.

'Hee hee! Bet he's back in the boat,' Jake said, again too loud. 'Won't be long now.'

It wasn't. The boat engine started purring and a minute later the reeds to the left of the boathouse began wagging madly and we could see that a tunnel was being carved through them. The engine died.

Jake was half standing. 'I can see the top of his head, his big clown's head,' he said.

'Keep down!' Gav hissed. 'He'll see us.'

'No, he won't. He's too thick.'

I was digging my fingernails into the palms of my hands.

The nose of the boat was just visible. It came slightly closer, then stopped.

'Bet he's grounded,' said Jake. 'He'll have to jump.'

We could hear Costigan clumping around in the boat. Then the reeds waved violently.

'It's really squishy just there. He'll get stuck,' Gav whispered.

'Only a thick would have landed the boat there!' Jake crowed.

Costigan came shoving his way through the reeds, lifting his boots high out of slurpy ground. Suddenly he gave a croaky shout and we clearly heard a seriously bad word.

Beside me Jake was sniggering and spluttering, 'What a thick! What a thick!'

Costigan was now balancing awkwardly on a hummock, preparing to jump to another hummock.

'He's in—' Gav started, but stopped as Costigan launched himself forward.

Next second we could just see his top half. His legs below his knees had vanished. He'd fallen short of the hummock and, slurp, landed in the squish.

'. . . trouble,' Gav finished.

Jake was banging his head on the ground, cracking up entirely. I gave him a shove.

'Shut up!' I said. 'It's not funny.'

Jake looked at me, his eyes wet. 'Not funny?' He looked from me to Costigan, then at Gav, then burst out laughing again.

Costigan was scrabbling at the grass on the hummock, trying to pull himself up again. It wasn't working.

'He's stuck,' Gav said. He stood up, looking really worried.

'Get down!' Jake grabbed Gav's jacket and tried to yank him down, but Gav pulled away. 'We've got to do something.'

'Don't be soft,' Jake said. 'Someone will come along and pull him out. I always thought he was a stick-in-the-mud anyway.'

Gav completely ignored him. 'Come on, Stephen,' he said and started moving down the slope. Jake reached out his hand to trip him, but Gav skipped away and was gone.

'Em,' I said, standing up, dithering. The last thing I wanted was to let Costigan see me.

'Lunatic,' Jake sneered. 'Gavvy-wavvy sucking up to Costigan as usual. He can't do anything anyway.'

That did it.

'Yes, he can!' I said. And I picked up the coil of rope and dashed after Gav.

Gav was calling to Mr Costigan, 'Hey, sir! Are you all right?'

Amazingly, Costigan gave us a big grin. 'It's Batman and Robin, I hope. I'm in a sticky situation here, lads.'

'Are you really stuck, sir?' I asked.

'Realio trulio. And it's extremely coldio.'

I was wondering if he'd lost his mind.

'If it isn't too much trouble, could you get me out of here? I reckon I'll survive another three or four minutes. After that, death, sure and certain.'

'What'll we do, sir?'

'Well, that handy piece of rope which you're holding, Stephen, and which I seem to recognize, could be put to a useful purpose.'

'Yes, sir?'

'See that metal hoop at the back of the car, near the exhaust pipe? Thread the rope through that.'

We did.

'That's it. Knot it again.'

We did, fiddling and foothering.

'Grand job. Now toss me the other end.'

We did. Costigan pulled the rope taut, then grinned at us. 'I hope I don't drag the car in on top of me. Then we'd all be in a right pickle.'

He heaved on the rope, scrunching up his face like a woman I saw on TV having a baby, and with a squelch hauled himself out. He stood gasping beside us, his trousers thick with mud.

'Oboysoboys!' he gasped. 'At least I escaped death. Until my wife sees these pants anyway.' He chuckled, then patted each of us on the shoulder. 'Thanks, Batman. Thanks, Robin.'

'Sir, were you not scared in there?' I asked. 'What if no one had been around?'

He chuckled again. 'Ah, sure, I knew someone would turn up. And if they didn't, I could always have used this.' He dipped his hand into his pocket and took out a mobile phone. 'Handy yokes when you're in a pickle. Lucky you were around though. Now I'd better do something about this boat.'

He put a hand in his pocket and took out a key which he waggled at us. 'By the way, one good turn cancels out a bad turn, so we'll forget about your practical joke.'

'Practical joke, sir?' Gav said, trying to sound surprised. His face was red and I knew mine was too.

'Ah now, who are you codding, boys? But you can tell that other creature I'll be calling to his house this evening.'

'Other creature, sir?' Gav said, still pretending, but making a very bad job of it.

Costigan chuckled. 'You know what I always say about eyes in the back of my head?'

We nodded.

'Well, today it was more a matter of eyes

in the front of my head.'

He unzipped his jacket and pulled out a pair of binoculars which were hanging round his neck on a cord.

'So tell Jake the rat I'll be calling to his house to give his slippery tail a good hard yank. Good luck now, boys.'

He walked to the boathouse, unlocked the padlock, opened the door and disappeared into the dark inside.

PAINTING
THE FACES OF
ANGELS

Mark O'Sullivan

'Your daddy is with the angels now, Seán,' Mam kept telling me, after the funeral. 'An angel in Heaven.'

I was ten years old – too old to believe in angels. Angels weren't six feet tall. They didn't have big, careless mops of hair so red it was almost orange. Angels didn't have sandy moustaches or brown eyes or a lovely high laugh that was like a song.

'We'll all meet again in Heaven some day,' she said. Her hair was wild and wispy in the light of the oil lamp. Tears flowed down her cheeks. She looked like she'd been caught in a rainstorm.

'No, we won't. I'll never see him again,' I insisted. 'I can't even see him in my head. I can't remember his face.'

And it was true. All our family photographs had been mislaid when we'd moved to Dun Laoghaire, a few months before. Without them, I couldn't make his face appear. I shut my eyes tight to concentrate on imagining him. All I could see was a blank greyness, like the heavy mist that had gathered over our seaside town.

The weeks passed in a long, slow silence.

All day, every day, the oil lamps burned in our small house. Outside, the mist licked the colours from shops and house fronts, from the carriage horses in the street, even from the faces of people. All that was left were dark shadows and grey shades.

All day, every day, I sat by my bedroom window trying to remember what Daddy looked like. Once, I saw a man passing along the street below. He was Daddy's height and had the same broad shoulders, but I couldn't see his face as he walked away into the gloom. That was how I felt about Daddy. He was walking away and wouldn't turn round so that I could see his face.

My eyes grew weak from clamping them shut so often, and from my tears. Each time I opened them, the colours in my bedroom seemed to have faded a little more. Until one morning I woke to find that I could see no colours at all.

On my bedside table, the red box filled with my prized possession had turned a filthy black. The yellow and blue of the curtains had drained away. The rainbow painting pinned to my wall was an arc of greys, one darker than the next.

My sadness turned to fear. I ran to the door, ready to scream out for Mam. But I stopped myself. How could I tell Mam about this strange turn of events? She was already so sad and upset. Sometimes I imagined she had become a child, crying and sighing instead of speaking. I would have to keep it to myself.

The bare boards of the stairs I descended on that fearful, colourless morning were not merely dark. They seemed, to my eyes, to be covered in soot. When I opened the kitchen door, everything I saw was dusted with the same black grime. Even Mam's face. Her skin looked old and dirty. I couldn't imagine ever wanting to touch her again. The milk bottle on the table seemed to be filled with grey ashes.

'I can't see his face,' she cried. 'I can't remember what he looked like.'

Not Mam too, I thought. I had to get away from there. My legs carried me weakly towards the hallway door. Behind me, Mam's sobs sang of heartbreak. I escaped into the misty street outside.

We had come to live in the lovely seaside town of Dun Laoghaire in June of that terrible year. Daddy got a new job in a paint shop there. He loved the work, mixing and selling all kinds of paint. House paints for inside and out; oils and watercolours for artists. And I loved the town. All summer, the long pier teemed with holiday makers and day trippers. The sun made waves of gold across the water and candyfloss crackled across my tongue like a sweet, pink frost. All along the seafront stood the grandest houses I had ever seen, their sloping gardens awash with flowers.

One August day, as we walked by those houses on our way to a Punch and Judy show on the pier, I asked Daddy what his favourite colour was.

'What's yours?' he asked, twiddling his sandy moustache in that funny way he had.

'Red!' I declared as another sugary mouthful of candyfloss melted on my tongue.

He turned to Mam and put his arm about her waist playfully.

'And what would the fair lady's choice be?'

'Don't be squeezing me on the street,' Mam tittered then considered the array of colours in the gardens above us. 'Yellow, I think. Yes, the yellow of those tulips up there.'

'That settles it then,' Daddy said. 'My favourite colour is orange.'

'Why, Daddy?'

'Because red is yours and yellow is your mother's. Mix the two and what do you get? Only orange.'

'Like your hair,' I joked because he preferred to call it gold.

'Go on out of that, you scamp,' he laughed, and tossed my hair with his big, soft hand.

But that was summer. That was before Daddy passed away in the deep of winter, before his face was hidden from me, before the colours died on me.

On that dismal morning, I walked from our street into the mist. Main Street was a haze of windows and doors, holding dark secrets. People emerged from the mist with a heart-stopping suddenness, grey and unreal. The bells of a tram rang eerily as I rushed across the street tracks. Behind its fogged-up windows, the passengers seemed like faceless ghosts. Like Daddy.

Down at the pier I was alone at last. Hidden in the mist, I saw neither the sea behind nor the grand houses before me. I sat on the cold ground. Every so often I walked up and down by the wall to warm myself. Once I even ran and when I was in full flight, I thought I heard Daddy's laugh. I stopped and the laughter was gone. I ran again but it didn't come back. There seemed no point in trying any more to remember Daddy's face. Instead, I found myself a deep puddle of water to mess about in. I saw my own dull reflection there and splashed it away angrily.

Then a gentle thud sounded from the other end of the pier. A woman's voice rang out through the mist.

'Well, blast it anyway!'

I chuckled to myself. I hadn't laughed since the funeral and it felt strange. To my astonishment, an orange bowled slowly along the ground from the heart of the mist. It tipped over into the puddle. I watched it float there, amazed that I could see its colour. I thought my black and white nightmare was over.

Filled with excitement, I walked towards the place from which the orange had come. In the thick of the fog I came upon an old woman dressed in black. I didn't see her face at first. She was very small and very annoyed with herself. Her string messages bag had split open. Bending stiffly, she snatched up a tin of sardines and a packet of tea from the wet footpath.

'I'll help you, missus,' I said.

She turned to look at me. My heart sank as I saw yet another face made ugly with greyness. I looked at the fruit in my hand. It was a grey, pock-marked thing.

'You're a gentleman,' she said. Her black-gloved hands trembled. Or maybe the gloves were blue or even red. How could I tell?

'I'll carry the bag for you,' I offered. 'Where do you live?'

'Just up the road here,' she said. 'I hope I'm not putting you out now.'

'I wasn't doing anything, anyway.'

I followed her to a gate leading into one of those grand, seafront houses. On the pillar, a plaque announced:

MRS KATHERINE FOGARTY

PHOTOGRAPHER

HAND-TINTING A SPECIALITY

'That's me,' the old woman declared. 'Aren't I very grand with my brass plaque?'

But I wasn't listening. I was wondering what hand-tinting was. Perplexed, I followed her up a steep path to the house. There, the old woman fumbled with her keys awhile before opening the front door and stepping into a large, dark hallway.

'Come on in and I'll find a sixpence for you,' she said.

'It's all right,' I told her. 'You don't have to pay me.'

'Sure, can't you come in anyway,' she insisted. 'I could do with a chat.' She walked on and, from the murky depths of the house, I heard her say, 'Close the door and don't be letting in the draught.'

The first room I passed through was a

photographic studio. A big box camera stood on a tripod. There was a long couch and, behind it, a huge painting of the pier jutting out into a dark sea beyond. Above the sea was a gloomy sky and a huge, pale moon. The second room was smaller and had no windows. At its centre was a table which left very little room to walk about. High timber shelves covered the walls from floor to ceiling. Each shelf had a small sign. I read some of them as the old woman made her way to a chair and sat down with a sigh:

Families: A to C. Couples: K to M. Singles: Men – P to T.

On the table lay piles of the black and white photographs the old woman had taken in her studio. She fished a sixpence from her handbag and held it out shakily towards me. Then she drew it back, staring at me oddly.

'I know your face from somewhere,' she said. 'What's your name?' Her curious gaze was making me uneasy now.

'Seán,' I told her warily.

'How would you like to earn a sixpence every day, Seán?' she asked.

I shrugged.

'You see, my hands are gone very shaky,' she explained. 'And I've an awful lot of work to catch up on. I could teach you how to hand-tint.'

'What's hand-tinting?'

'Well, people like to put some colour in their photographs,' she said. 'It makes them more real, more alive. So, I paint the sea and the sky and the faces and . . .'

Suddenly, I felt angry. I didn't mean to say anything but it just flooded out of me. 'You can't make a face more alive if it's dead, if it's gone and it won't come back,' I cried. 'Like Daddy's.'

I turned to run from her. As I did I saw, high up on the shelves, a sign I hadn't noticed before. *Angels*, it read. My curiosity was stirred but my need to get away was stronger. I ran towards the door.

'Wait, Seán. I know exactly how you feel,' the old woman called, 'Please, come back.'

I ran all the way home. I found Mam crying in the kitchen. I thought that for the rest of our lives, we would be lonely, sad and grey.

Many weeks passed before I returned to Mrs Fogarty's house. The mist still shrouded Dun Laoghaire on the day I found my way back to her. My world was still a black and white one, and Daddy's face was still hidden from me. And from Mam.

What brought me back to that cavernous house? The distant memory of that orange floating in a puddle? The curious sign proclaiming *Angels*? The old woman's claim that she knew *exactly* how I felt? Maybe I was just tired of sitting alone at the pier and listening to the ghostly whisper of the sea.

Whatever the reason, I went back there not just once but every day for weeks on end. Mrs Fogarty must have thought me the oddest boy she'd ever met but she was too kind ever to say so. I arrived at her door and followed her inside day after day – and didn't speak a word as I watched her at work on her hand-tinting.

She would open her neat little watercolour box as soon as I'd settled on a chair opposite her. There were sixteen squares of colours – all of them shades of grey to me, of course. Very slowly and shakily, she painted the sky and clouds. Then the sea, the pier and the moon. From there she moved on to the clothes – suits and shirts, dresses and hats. Then, very carefully, she painted the hands. Only when every other detail was finished, did she start on the face. And the face always took a long, long time. Sometimes she spoke softly and it was always some curious lesson on faces. One day she asked, 'Did you ever hear of Leonardo da Vinci?'

I nodded. I'd learned about him in school; an artist and inventor.

'Well, he made out there's two hundred and fifty-six types of noses,' she said. 'Imagine that, Seán.'

I pretended not to listen but I loved to hear all those odd details. The little dimpled vale between the nose and the upper lip was called the philtrum, she told me. Human beings were the only animal with chins. People blink about fifteen times a minute.

'Isn't that a good one!' she declared. 'Is it any wonder my poor eyes get so blinking tired, ha ha!'

When she finished a photograph, she sat back so wearily, I thought she might fall asleep. Then one day she actually did drop off. That was the day I began to paint.

I had been watching Mrs Fogarty very closely. I knew exactly which squares of watercolour she dipped her brush in and mixed for each item – the sky, the sea, the moon. Though I saw only greys, I knew the exact shade of grey that was needed each time. She had let me stay there silently for so long, I felt I owed her something in return. I painted three photographs very quickly for her. It came easily to me. Except for the hands and face, which took so long I was sure she'd wake and catch me.

Soon Mrs Fogarty stirred. She stared at the photographs. I was afraid I'd messed them up but her smile alone told me that I hadn't. I felt so happy that the question I had been longing to ask slipped from my tongue.

'Why is that shelf marked *Angels*, Mrs Fogarty?'

'Oh, my Angels, they're the hardest of all to do,' she said. 'My Angels are the photographs of people who have passed away, Seán.' Her grey, wrinkled hand touched my shoulder. I didn't shrink from her.

'And do you know what, Seán?' she said. 'I think you're ready to paint the face of an Angel.'

My heart thumped in my chest. I couldn't speak. My eyes followed her as she went and reached up to the *Angels* shelf. She turned. In one hand she held a photograph of a man; in the other, a small, flat, wooden box.

'Do you remember the first day we met and I told you I knew your face?'

I nodded.

'That was because you look so like your father, Seán,' she explained.

My head was spinning so much I thought I might faint.

'You see, I used to buy my paints from him,' she said. 'And one day he came here with some new ones for me to try out and I took his photograph. I never got the chance to give it to him. It's yours now. And the paints too. I never used them.'

She placed the photograph before me. I couldn't look at it because I thought my heart would break when I saw Daddy. She opened the new box of watercolours.

'I can't,' I said weakly.

'There's not a thing in the world to be afraid of,' she said. 'Listen, Seán, our eyes are not just cameras. We don't just make old black and white pictures of the people we love and stack them away on some shelf in our minds and take them out when we want to remember them. No, when it comes to remembering, we're all artists painting our own memories. We use colours, sounds, feelings. Close your eyes, Seán.'

It felt strange but I did as she asked. I listened to her voice, soft as the hiss and murmur of the sea.

'Imagine a lovely summer's day, Seán. Feel the heat of the sun on your back. Hear the laughing, splashing sounds down on the beach. See the colours of the beach chairs, the blue and yellow and green. See the red and white stripes of the Punch and Judy booth.' She spoke more softly still, each word a sigh like a wave foaming on the shore. 'Feel. Listen. See. Remember. Make your own memories, Seán, paint your own memories of your daddy. That way you can never lose them.'

I opened my eyes. No sooner had the first dab of grey paint touched the photograph than it shone out in all its sky-blueness. I went excitedly on. The bright, white cloud had a hint of red in it. The ripples on the blue sea were tinged with a deep yellow. And that big ball in the sky was no moon now. It was a bright orange sun. My right hand shook so much as I painted Daddy's hands, that I had to hold it steady with the left. With every stroke of lightest peach colour, I could feel his strong but tender touch.

Memories came rushing back, of that day when we talked about our favourite colours. Real memories that I could feel and see and hear. I felt his hand brushing my hair and the taste of candyfloss was so real that my mouth watered. I saw the big, careless mop of hair so red it was almost orange. I saw the sandy moustache and the dancing brown eyes. I heard the song of his big, high laugh as I ran home to Mam with the photograph. And a vast orange sun burned away the mist from over Dun Laoghaire and from our grey lives.

THE HARP

Larry O'Loughlin

Downstairs, he could hear his father singing as he got himself ready for work. Danny knew the song, 'Bold Fenian Men'. They never had parties in his house, but if they did then that'd be the song his dad would have sung. He was always singing or humming it. Danny listened.

'It was down by the Glenside I heard a young maid sing,' sang his dad.

'Glory-o, Glory-o to the bold Fenian men,' Danny sang along quietly.

He heard his father's footsteps moving towards the front door. The singing stopped. The door opened and he heard his father offer a shy, mumbled 'Morning,' to someone passing as he stepped out on to the pavement. Then the door closed quietly.

Danny rolled over and checked the clock on the tallboy. He didn't need to do it. If his father had left for work then it was five forty-five. He left at the same time every morning. He'd worked in the same factory for twenty-five years and he'd never been late.

'We're like a team,' he'd told Danny once. 'We depend on each other. If I'm late there's no one to pull the metal out of the furnace and the whole team is let down.' Danny hadn't really understood that, but he'd nodded anyway.

He eased himself noiselessly out of bed and stood up. His bed was in the corner of his parents' room. His three sisters shared another room and the tiny box-room was normally occupied by some uncle who'd come over from Ireland looking for work. His mother turned in her sleep, mumbling something about 'Johnny'. He froze. If she woke she'd send him straight back to bed and he had to be up early this morning. He wasn't going to let Kevin McCrory lord it over him today.

'I hate Kevin McCrory, the big show-off,' he told himself silently.

He waited for a few seconds until he could hear his mother softly snoring, then he lifted his clothes and boots off the floor and tiptoed to the door. He was freezing. The house was like an ice-box. He stopped and looked at her again. She seemed to be smiling in her sleep. He couldn't be sure, but he guessed that she was dreaming of being back in Dublin, probably up to some scrape or other with her brother, Uncle Johnny. She'd been living in Birmingham for twenty-five years, ever since his dad had got the job and sent for her, but Danny knew that, in her heart, his mother had never really left Dublin. She carried the city somewhere in her soul and every night and most days she managed to slip back there for a while.

His dad was different. His dad didn't miss it at all. 'How can you miss a place that drives you out at twenty because at twenty-one they'd have to pay you the wages of a man?' he'd heard him complain at times. 'If I never go back it'll be too soon. This is my country now.'

Yet every night he'd go up to his bedroom and try to get Radio Éireann on his old radio. Every Sunday he'd give Danny the money to buy the *Irish Press* newspaper and *Ireland's Own* magazine from the man who sold papers outside the church and every July, when the car factories closed down for two weeks, Danny's family would be among the thousands of other families heading to Holyhead for the boat 'home'.

Danny tiptoed down the stairs, praying that his sisters wouldn't be up before him. He didn't think they would, but he prayed anyway. It was 17 March 1957. In two days' time he'd be nine, the same age as Kevin McCrory, but right at that moment that didn't matter. What mattered was that today was St Patrick's Day, the most important day in the school year and he was going to make sure that Kevin McCrory wouldn't be able to sneer at him again.

He was going to make sure that he, Danny Delaney, had a metal harp with green ribbons – the most important St Patrick's Day symbol in the school and one that Kevin McCrory always had.

He hadn't actually known how important St Patrick's Day was until yesterday. He'd known it was important but he'd always thought that Easter Sunday or Christmas Day were *the* days of the year. Then yesterday, after his class had practised singing 'Hail Glorious St Patrick, Dear Saint of Our Isle' for what seemed like the five thousandth time, Miss Flanagan had fixed them all with a menacing glare from her one good eye and warned, 'I don't care how much shamrock or how many rosettes and harps you wear on St Patrick's Day. It's the most important day of the year. So I expect to see you all at Holy Communion.'

At the word 'harps' Kevin McCrory had turned round and beamed at them all. Then he'd breathed on to his fingernails and rubbed them on his chest, a gesture designed to show that he had one up on the rest of them.

'And woe betide anyone who isn't at Communion,' bellowed Miss Flanagan. 'Do you understand?'

'Yes, Miss,' the class had responded in terror, but Danny had been thinking more about metal harps.

Danny reached the door at the bottom of the stairs and knocked on it softly, three short raps; just enough to scare off any stray mice. He hated mice almost as much as he hated Kevin McCrory. He pushed the door open and switched on the light. On the table there was half a pan loaf, a small block of butter and a bread knife. Without thinking, he cut off a chunk of bread, buttered it and took a bite. Before he could swallow it he remembered Miss Flanagan. He spat the bread out in terror and raced to the sink to rinse any crumbs from his mouth. You couldn't go to Communion if you'd eaten beforehand.

He walked from the kitchen into the living room and dressed himself quickly. He was still freezing. He went to the front room and looked out. It was dark. There was hardly anyone around. He'd never been up this early before, but today he had no choice.

Today, every single kid in school, Spanish and Italians included, would be walking around with enough shamrock pinned to their jumpers to cover a small farm. Some of the girls would be wearing green ribbons in their hair. Most of the kids would be wearing green, white and gold rosettes. ('We look like we're all Shamrock Rovers supporters,' Johnny Burke had laughed the previous year.) But some, just a few and mainly the eldest kids in a family, would be wearing the most treasured badge of them all: a small metal harp with green ribbons on it. Kevin McCrory certainly would and Danny intended to be as well.

Most kids in his school had their shamrock and badges sent to them by family in Ireland. Danny's Auntie Mary always sent theirs, but because the harp was expensive she only ever sent one harp and three rosettes. It was OK for the likes of Kevin McCrory and Paddy Maguire. They were the eldest in their families. They always got first choice, but Danny was the baby of his family, though he hated that word 'baby'. His three sisters were older and now that Marie had been working for two years, the choice of who got the harp was between Gina or Breda, unless . . .

Danny watched the people passing outside the front window. As the time moved towards half six their numbers grew. Most were dressed like his dad: flat cap, mac, scarf and big, steel-toed boots. Some carried their sandwiches and flask of tea in little shopping bags, others used the same sort of khaki bag his dad used. They'd carried gas masks in them during the war.

He watched the steady procession of boys heading down towards the dairy at the bottom of his street. He'd probably work there when he was older, unless he joined his dad in the car factory. The boys were wearing their working clothes. The ones wearing brown smock-coats under their macs worked on the milk carts with milkmen, bringing milk to the houses. The ones who helped the lorry men to bring the crates of milk to the shops were wearing blue overalls and Wellington boots. He didn't know why they wore Wellingtons, maybe in case they dropped the crates and the bottles broke. He knew a lot of the boys. Some of the older ones, the boys who'd left two years ago with his sister Marie, gave him a wave or winked at him as they passed. The younger ones, the ones who'd left school at Christmas, just walked past, taking extra long puffs on their cigarettes, trying to look important.

A few minutes later, Danny heard the soft clip-clop of horses' hooves and the soft tinkle of bottles as the milk carts left the dairies and deliveries began. But he wasn't interested in the milkmen. He was waiting for the postman. If he could be the one to get Auntie Mary's package first, he could get the harp and pin it on his jumper before his sisters were even awake. He knew if he did that they wouldn't dare to take it off him. If they did, he'd scream the house down and his mother would give out to them. Being the baby had some advantages. It was a perfect plan.

The milkmen came and went and soon the street was alive with other people heading off to work. Danny shivered with the cold. It was so cold he could see his breath rising in front of him like smoke. He wanted to go back to bed to keep warm, but he couldn't risk it.

How he hated Kevin McCrory. It was his fault he was cold. He checked his watch. Half seven. The postman better come soon otherwise his sisters would be up. He pressed his nose against the window and looked up and down the road. No sign of him.

At a quarter to eight, Danny opened the door and stepped out on to the freezing street. He looked down towards the dairy and then up towards the pub.

Nothing! He quickly went back inside.

Five minutes later, he grabbed his duffel coat from the back of the door and went out and sat on the step, looking up and down. He heard the door of the house next to his open.

'Happy St Patrick's Day, Danny Boy,' smiled Mr Broadbent as he stepped out on to the footpath. 'You're up early.'

'Happy St Patrick's Day, Mr Broadbent,' Danny replied. 'I'm just waiting for the shamrock to arrive.'

'Aunt's late this year then, Dan?' said Mr Broadbent. He looked at Danny with a twinkle in his eye, 'Or are you hoping to get your pick before the girls get up?'

Danny blushed.

'I had three big sisters myself,' smiled Mr Broadbent. 'Flipping right nuisances.' Then he pulled his cap out of his pocket and jammed it on to his head. 'Got to go. The beer won't bottle itself. Don't stay there too long. You'll catch your death and you were sick only the other week.'

'I won't.'

Even with his coat on, Danny was freezing. He felt himself begin to snuffle, so he went back inside and took his place at the window. He could hear movement upstairs. Flip! His sisters were beginning to stir.

'Please! Please! Please! Come,' he pleaded, looking out of the window. 'Please.'

His sisters would be down any minute. He looked up the road again and nearly jumped through the window. The postman was just emerging from under the railway bridge and turning into the street. Danny opened the door and raced out to meet him.

'Anything for Delaney's at one hundred and forty-two?'

The postman looked into his bag. 'Just this,' he said, taking out the envelope from Littlewoods pools. 'Just the pools coupon for your dad.'

'You couldn't look again, could you?' asked Danny, taking the envelope.

'Expecting something important?'

'Yes.'

The postman checked through the bag again. 'Sorry, I haven't got anything else for you.' He turned and walked off.

Danny couldn't believe it. Auntie Mary always sent the shamrock every year. She couldn't have forgotten.

'Are you sure?' he called after the postman.

'Certain,' the postman called back.

Danny walked back up to the house. He could almost hear Kevin McCrory sneering at him. He walked into the living room and put the envelope on the table.

He looked at the bread beside it. Right! There was only one thing to do. He picked up the hunk of bread and started chewing it.

'What're you doing?' screeched Gina, coming down the stairs into the room. 'You can't go to Communion now. Old bat-eye Flanagan will go mad.'

'I'm not going to school, achoo,' said Danny, faking a sneeze. 'I feel sick.' Then he sneezed again. Large chunks of bread flew out of his mouth.

'You little slob, I—' Gina began. Then she stopped and ran to the stairs.

'Mam, Danny's having a nosebleed.'

Danny almost smiled. A nosebleed! He was sneezing and having nosebleeds. Perfect. He'd no idea where the nosebleed had come from, but he didn't care. His mam wouldn't send him to school now. He wouldn't even have to pretend any more. He could spend the day in bed reading his comics, with his mam bringing him sweets and lemonade, while Kevin McCrory would be starving till after Mass and then spend the day shivering in school. 'Serves him right.' Tomorrow, Danny could go back to school and lie his head off about how sad he was that he couldn't come in, because he'd had the biggest and best harp ever and no one would know the difference. He couldn't have planned it better.

His mother sat him down in a chair, tipped his head back and put a cold key against the back of his neck to stop the bleeding.

'You just sit there like that for a while, love. You'll be grand.'

After a few seconds the bleeding stopped.

'Right,' she said, looking at him. 'Back to bed.'

Danny stood up and picked up his comics from the chair on which he'd left them the previous night.

'Put those back,' his mother ordered.

'But, Mam,' said Danny, surprised.

'No buts. I'm not having you sitting up reading and getting another heavy flu. I want you sleeping all day, and I'll bring up the jar.'

'No!' Danny almost screamed at the thought. 'Not the jar.' The 'jar' was a new water bottle his dad had bought. It was like a large flask, only made of metal and it got so hot when the hot water was poured into it that if you accidentally touched it, it was like putting your feet in the fire. And it didn't matter how many towels or blankets you covered it with, your feet always managed to fine one uncovered spot.

Her next sentence was even worse.

'And I'll dose you with Dr Gubbins's special cough mix.'

Danny could feel his stomach churning at the thought. Dr Gubbins was the local doctor and his belief seemed to be that the worse a medicine smelled, and the more horrible it tasted, then the better it was for you. All his medicine was revolting but the cough medicine was the worst ever. It was sticky and slimy, smelled revolting and tasted even worse. Peter Foley said it was made from rats' wee and dogs' droppings melted in treacle. It tasted like it.

'I'm feeling OK now,' Danny panicked. 'I really am.' Kevin McCrory could laugh at him all day. He didn't mind. Anything was better than the jar and the cough mix.

'I feel a whole lot . . . achoo!' he sneezed again, but this time the sneeze came all on its own. 'I'm OK . . . achoo . . . I just . . . achooo.'

'That settles it, me lad. Bed. Now!' his mother ordered.

Danny moved across the room miserably. Just as he reached the bottom of the stairs he heard a soft tapping at the letter-box.

'I'll get it,' offered Breda.

Danny heard her opening the door and saying, 'Thanks.'

'Look,' she chirped excitedly, turning from the door, waving a box as big as a small box of biscuits. 'Special Delivery from Auntie Mary.'

As his sister tore eagerly at the wrapping, Danny's stomach sank.

It couldn't be. He sat down on the stairs.

Gina and his mother crowded around as Breda lifted the lid off the box.

'Look,' said Gina, as if the other two couldn't see exactly what she was seeing. 'She's sent us a special Patrick's Day cake . . . and these.'

She held up three large, gleaming metal harps with green, white and orange ribbon streaming from them. Much better than anything Kevin McCrory had ever had.

Danny felt like crying. He stood up and walked to the table. Maybe the cake would cheer him up. It was iced with green icing and there was a large shamrock on it. Underneath the shamrock, someone had written, 'St Patrick's Day 1957'. Danny licked his lips. It looked delicious. 'I bet Kevin McCrory won't have anything like this today,' he grinned to himself. He picked up the knife and started to cut himself a large slice.

'What do you think you're doing?' asked his mother.

'It's OK. I'm not going to Communion so I can have some.'

His mother shook her head. 'Oh, no you can't,' she said firmly. 'You can't eat for two hours before or after Dr Gubbins's medicine.'

Danny couldn't believe it. He was stunned. He flopped on to a chair. He had only one thought on his mind:

I HATE KEVIN – ROTTEN – MCCRORY.

OUR DOGS

Carlo Gébler

I was eight. It was the last day of the summer term. I walked back to our suburban London house with its knobby front of white pebble-dash.

The door was on the latch. I pushed and went in. Two cardboard suitcases stood in the hall. I tested them; yes, they were packed. We were going on our long-anticipated holiday. But only my brother and I. I examined the luggage labels to confirm this. They were handwritten in ink in my father's odd, cramped script. Conor was written on one, Michael on the other, plus our address. Michael, my six-year-old brother was already home; infants finished before juniors. He got back from school an hour before I did.

'The soap's in my eyes,' my brother screeched behind the kitchen door.

He was having his hair washed at the kitchen sink. Our mother always washed our hair before we went away.

'Use the facecloth,' my mother said.

I crept down the corridor and, without my mother seeing, turned into the dining room. With its black and white linoleum floor tiles it was like a gigantic chessboard. My *Nine Starlight Tales* by Alison Uttley was on the sideboard.

I took the book and slipped out through the French doors to the verandah at the back.

'Stay still,' I heard my mother saying. She did not enjoy washing our hair any more than we did.

I ran to the coal bunker halfway down the garden. It had two chambers, but we only ever used one. I climbed up and dropped through the hatch into the other, the one that was always empty. It was clean and chilly and completely silent in there. I looked up through the open hatchway at the square of blue above. Bliss. My very own desert island.

It couldn't last and it didn't.

'Conor,' I heard. My brother's face appeared between the sky and me. His hair was wet and his eyes were red. 'Mum wants you. You've got to have your hair washed.'

She wanted to send us clean and scrubbed to her mother's house. I didn't understand why, just that this was how it had to be.

I took my book, clambered on to the bunker roof and jumped down on to the path. The clasps of my sandals jingled.

'I hate having my hair washed,' I said.

'Conor, stop dawdling,' my mother called from the kitchen door.

I walked towards the house, as if towards my own execution.

The next day we drove to the airport, my father, my mother, my brother and I. My father was silent. My mother sniffled. The night before when she kissed me goodnight she said, 'I want you to go to Granny's but I want you to stay as well, you know. I'll be heartbroken without you and Michael.' That's what it was to be grown-up; you wanted this but you also wanted that. It was called 'being torn'. I, on the other hand, felt pure, uncomplicated happiness as we sped towards Heathrow. Eight weeks on my grandparents' farm in the west of Ireland lay ahead. Liberty Hall. I could hardly wait.

We were brought into the terminal building and led to the desk with Aer Lingus written over it. A lady with red lipstick hung name-tags on chains round our necks.

'Now say goodbye to your mummy and daddy,' she said.

''Bye,' my brother lisped.

''Bye,' I said. I could barely speak. I was too excited. After weeks of waiting it really was happening at last. We were on our way.

My mother's eyes, I saw, were wet. I

couldn't look at her. I didn't want to. The stewardess opened a door.

'Go on,' our mother said.

We scooted through. The door closed. Thank goodness. No more wet eyes now. We followed the stewardess down a corridor, across tarmac rank with the smell of fuel, and up steps into a sleek, silver airplane. On take-off I went deaf, and some two or three hours later, bumping down at Shannon, I heard popping in my ear. Then I heard the metal steps on wheels being trundled to the door.

'You can go first,' said a different stewardess. We bolted out of the door into an Irish summer's afternoon. A breeze blew and there were big white clouds marooned in the sky.

Grandmother was waiting in the wooden terminal, dressed in a purple hat and a black fur coat with a sealskin collar, her posh coat that she wore winter and summer at all important events.

'Are you well?' she asked solemnly.

'Yes.'

Mr Dolan, the local hackney car driver, was beside her. His squashed-up eyes reminded me of raisins. He carried our bags outside. His car, a black Humber, had newspaper over the front windscreen to stop the sun heating it up.

'Can we go in the front?' we chorused together.

'No,' said my granny.

We got in the back. She was in the middle. There was a smell of Sweet Afton tobacco and her scent, Evening in Paris.

Mr Dolan climbed in, turned the key and pulled away with extreme caution, then drove slowly eastwards. Other cars made him nervous. Only nearing our neighbourhood, where there were almost no cars, did he relax.

'Are they safe?' he asked suddenly, his voice as deliberate as his driving.

'What do you mean?' my grandmother asked.

'Planes.'

'Don't be putting ideas in their heads,' she said.

We turned a corner and saw the gates of the house. They were black and stood open. Beyond, a tree-lined avenue stretched to my grandparents' granite house at the end.

Mr Dolan edged between the piers and began to slowly bump forward. We looked through the window. Where were the dogs? Why weren't they barking? Why couldn't we see two brown blobs bolting out from under the box-hedge that encased the house and hurtling pell-mell down the lawn towards us? That's what they did whenever a car appeared, they ran riot. They came down to the gate. They followed the car back to the house. And then, frantic with excitement, they jumped up and licked your face when you got out. Rover and Dixie they were called. We didn't have dogs at home. It was not right to have big animals in a small house in the city. But here, we always found them waiting as if they wanted the holiday as much as we did. Except today, they were nowhere to be seen. They were gone.

'The dogs,' we said. I was sick. So was Michael. I feared the worst. They no longer lived here.

My grandmother cleared her throat. She always made this noise when she didn't like what she had to say.

'Well, lads, the dogs,' she said.

'Lads'. This was not a word she used much. Yes, I was right to expect the worst. She'd banished them, I decided, as she'd sometimes threatened in the past, because she was too old and they were too much trouble.

'Rover and Dixie have gone to sleep,' she said.

'Can we wake them up?' said my brother hopefully.

'No,' my grandmother said.

This was worse than the worst. If we didn't have them, how could we have a holiday?

'They're in the fairy fort,' she said. 'I'll show you later.'

After tea, she took us into the circle of hawthorns at the back of the kitchen garden and showed us two mounds, each with a cross made from twigs tied together. To be told was one thing but to see the earth heaps was another. With my mind's eye I saw myself, my brother and the dogs the previous summer, laughing in the haggard as we tumbled in the coarse, brass-coloured old hay, then chasing through the ragwort with its strange metal smell at the end of the avenue.

We filed back to the house in silence. My granny went inside. I fetched our pretend rifles from the metal shed and we attempted a game of war. Chasing up and down the box-hedge, I passed several hollows lined with brown fur. The dogs had made them, of course. Recently, I guessed. Then I remembered that the mounds in the fairy ring were bare. I realized they weren't long dead. Once I had that thought, my heart went right off the game.

'Come on,' I said to my brother. His heart wasn't in it either.

We went and climbed the old oak halfway

up the path to the yard. It was evening now and butter-coloured sunlight slanted horizontally across the countryside. I thought about Rover and Dixie. Michael did as well, I imagine. I felt sad, really sad suddenly and I wished at that moment I was back with my own mother.

Jemmy, the farmhand, appeared. He carried a gallon pail. The evening's milking, I guessed, was just finished.

'Lads,' he said breezily, as if the year that had passed since he last saw us had never happened and we'd spoken only the evening before.

'What happened to the dogs?' my brother asked.

Jemmy stopped at the foot of the tree and looked up at us swinging our feet. We both wore sandals with a sunflower pattern of holes over the toes.

'The creamery sent a new driver. He reversed over them.' Jemmy said this matter-of-factly, bluntly, but then that was how he always was about animals. I wasn't surprised, yet what I took as his indifference made me feel even sadder still.

In the evening we sat around the Aga in the kitchen. My granny asked questions. We answered them without enthusiasm. I had a strong, hot pain at the top of my stomach and a soreness at the back of my throat. I felt like crying. Michael sounded the same. My grandmother saw this for she went off and came back with our grandfather. He was a tall man in a three-piece suit. He had been in the front room since we arrived, smoking and reading one of his many books about horse breeding.

'Would you like to see my fob?' he said in a mild voice I never remembered him using before. We didn't answer. He pulled the heavy gold watch from his waistcoat pocket. There was a picture of the Statue of Liberty on the front. He opened the lid to show the face, and the tune of 'Yankee Doodle' trilled from inside the gold case.

We nodded. Though it had thrilled us the previous summer, this time it didn't. How could we be excited about anything when the only things that really mattered, the dogs, were gone?

Grandfather couldn't fail to notice our unexpected indifference. 'All righty,' he said. 'This should cheer you up.'

He gave each of us a lovely Irish half-crown. It was a lot of money, he knew that. We said, 'Thank you,' politely but without feeling. Grandfather, his cheering-up duties done, returned to the front room and his books.

'Put the money in the Fyson's box,' said Granny. She pointed at the tin with the slit on the window ledge where she always made us keep our change.

One after the other we obediently dropped our money in. As our coins crashed to the bottom they struck other coins.

'I already put money in there for you,' she explained. 'You can go to Conway's shop tomorrow, if you like.'

We agreed we could and sat down again.

Silence.

'All right,' said Grandmother after a bit. 'There isn't anything else – only the one thing that'll please you two, is there?'

What did she mean? They were gone, weren't they? And then I had a fantastic idea. It was too good to be true.

'But have you any idea,' she continued, 'what it means? You get them and they're puppies and they're sweet and naughty.'

My intuition was right.

'Then they grow up,' she said. 'You get used to them. They grow into you. You grow into them. They're always there. In the morning when you come out, they're at the door. Last thing at night, when you bolt the kitchen door, they're on the flagstones at the back, and after you're in you hear them getting into their hollows under the box-hedge for the night. Yes, you love them – and then what happens?' She banged her hand on the table. 'They go, they're gone. It hurts. And they're only dogs. Dogs. Not people. And you want me to go through what I've just been through again?'

It was the longest and strongest speech I had ever heard her make.

'Well?' She looked at us. 'What have you got to say?'

I knew what I wanted to say. *Yes*, I wanted to say. *Yes, please, can we, can we, can we? It would make our holiday. It would mean everything*. But how could I say what I wanted after what I'd just heard? I couldn't.

'I want Rover and Dixie,' I heard my brother say solemnly. He was still young enough to say what he felt, exactly as he felt it. I, on the other hand, was losing that, if I hadn't already lost it.

My grandmother sighed, looked at Michael and then back at me. 'Get my writing box, Conor. Let's see what we can do.'

I opened the press. It smelled of flour. I took the ancient box printed with a rose pattern and carried it to the table where my grandmother sat cleaning her glasses.

'Do you know what?' she said. She opened the box and took out the Basildon

Bond writing pad. 'Writing makes me sick.' She opened the pad and smoothed the top sheet. 'I'm not promising. How can I when I don't know what Mr Gilmore has?'

She laboriously copied her address along the top of the page.

'If he has them, good and fine. He may still have the breeding pair that gave us Rover and Dixie. But if he hasn't, well, don't say I didn't warn you.'

The next morning I handed the letter to the postman along with a coin for him to buy a stamp to put on it. The following day a boy in a uniform cycled up the drive. He went to the front door and pulled the bell. I was in the kitchen reading an ancient *Dandy* annual. I heard my grandfather grumbling in the hall and pulling the front door open. It was awkward because the door was rarely used. A few moments later he came into the kitchen with a cream envelope.

'Telegram – yours.'

My grandmother, kneading bread on the table, was white with flour to the elbows.

'Read it.'

' "Last bus from Limerick tomorrow afternoon. Gilmore." '

We were down at our gate at five that next afternoon though the bus never passed before half-past at the earliest. It was raining and we huddled under one of grandfather's old umbrellas. It was torn in two places and the warm summer rain dripped through, splashing our shoulders, or trickling down our bare legs and running into our Wellington boots.

I looked down the road. I saw thick, grey rods of rain falling from the sky, the tar macadam shining with wet, and the sodden fuchsia hedgerow curving into the corner round which the bus would appear.

'Will it come?' my brother asked.

'It will. It always comes.' Hadn't we often stood on just this spot on a Thursday waiting for the bus to come with comics for Conway's shop?

I strained my ears for the sound of the heavy tyres sloshing along. A man appeared, driving an old grey donkey loaded with kerosene cans.

'Get out of my road,' he hissed, though we were well out of his way, and he hurried on by.

'A bad man,' my brother whispered.

The rain went on falling. Nothing stirred except the crows in the big tree behind. A dog barked up on the bog, the noise it made was mournful. My arm began to ache from holding the umbrella, the feet in my Wellington's felt old. Could the bus, for once, have been early? Could we have missed it? Could that be possible? Or was it cancelled? Or had it crashed? Or broken down?

I would count to a hundred. When I got to a hundred I would suggest we retraced our steps to the house. I started counting inwardly while Michael moaned and sighed quietly at my side as he did when he was sad. I got to eighty-seven when I thought, yes, I heard something.

I held my breath. There, faraway, the putt-putt hurumph of an engine.

'I hear it,' said Michael.

We stared at the dripping fuchsia corner and waited and waited. The noise got louder and louder. Then, suddenly, the snub-nosed front of the city bus came round the corner, huge wipers surging across its enormous windscreen, the small figure of the driver crouched over the wheel behind.

I raised my hand and ran forward and he raised a finger in acknowledgement. The hiss of the brakes started and the great lumbering bus ground to a halt and the door opened. We looked up the steps at the driver, Mr Donnelly. He had black hair and a funny face. The left side moved, the right side didn't. He'd had polio as a child since when it was frozen.

'It's in the boot,' he said. 'I'll open it for you from here.'

He tugged a lever.

I thrust the open umbrella into Michael's arms. 'Here,' I said. I ran down the length of the bus, half aware of the faces staring down through the rain-spattered windows. Michael followed. At the back I lifted the wet boot door and there, at last, was the object for which we had waited and waited. It was a brown cardboard box with round breathing holes in the top that were made with a biro, and a label in one corner with my grandmother's name written on it. Something inside the box trembled and whined, and moved in the darkness below the breathing holes.

I took out the box and slammed the boot door. I ran back towards the front.

'Me, me, me carry,' Michael said, trailing behind. He spoke in the baby voice he put on when there was something he wanted desperately.

We reached the door and I looked up at the driver on his throne.

'You got it?' Mr Donnelly called. I showed him the box.

He nodded. The door closed, the brakes hissed and the bus pulled away.

'We'll carry it together,' I said.

I took the umbrella back and raised it. We began to walk. I held one end, my brother the other. It was awkward but fair. We went straight up the avenue and into the house by the back door. My grandmother was waiting in the kitchen.

'It came,' she said. 'Don't open it yet.' She put down yellowing sheets from the *Clare Champion* on the floor.

'Go on. Open the box now,' she said when she was done.

In the box the scrabbling was frantic. The box shook with it. We cut the string tied round it with the black scissors, its blades dark with old turkey blood. Then Michael and I lifted the lid off and looked down. Inside the box, two brown balls of tweed were rollicking in wood shavings and sawdust. Each stopped to look up for a second and then they both scaled the cardboard walls and flopped down on the other side.

My brother laughed. The puppies ran straight off the newspaper and on to the tiled floor. Here they immediately produced two warm pools of thin yellow water.

'They're just across the threshold and they've started,' my grandmother complained. Further pages from the *Clare Champion* were thrown over the puddles.

'Come here,' she said, gruffly. The puppies froze. She bent forward, her skirt riding up to show her varicose veins, the blue wormy twists that stuck up under her pale white skin.

'Let's see what you're made of.'

She took a puppy in each hand and turned it upside down.

'Ah. This one with the white nose we'll call Dixie,' she said, shaking the puppy at us, 'she's the girl, and this is Rover, the boy. Now, is it raining?'

She squinted out of the window. 'No, it's stopped. You go on out with Rover and Dixie and I never want to see a long face on either of you again like I've had to put up with these last days.'

She set the dogs on the floor. They skittered off towards the back door and slithered down the steps.

'And just remember, when they go, as they will, they'll break your hearts.'

We ignored her and, laughing, surged down the steps after our new friends.

Interesting things you probably didn't know about the authors . . .

Herbie Brennan

On last count, Herbie Brennan discovered he'd written ninety-one books so he decided to take a rest by contributing to this anthology. He is driven to write by the need to feed eight cats (with more on the way) and support a bad computer habit. Herbie lives in Ireland and devotes much of his time to the study of prehistory, which is how he knew so much about the life and times of Stone-Age Peig.

Stephanie Dagg

Loves: writing, reading, swimming, chocolate, the Internet.
Hates: housework, cooking, paying bills.
Family: married to Chris, a computer whizz. Three children – Benjamin who loves planes, animals and Goosebumps; Caitlín who adores kittens, make-up and Barbie;

and Ruadhri Stephen who was born just after this story was written. Also two hairy dogs.

Hobbies: knitting and gardening (but not at the same time).

To find out more, visit her website at *www.booksarecool.net*

Polly Devlin

Polly Devlin was born and grew up in rural Ireland and has one husband, three daughters, five sisters, one brother, eight dogs, sixteen self-shearing sheep, two horses, two Highland cattle, a pig called Duncan, odd hens, many calling birds and a farm which has become a nature haven and an SSSI (Site of Special Scientific Interest). She has written six books, all of them in different genres. She was awarded the OBE for services to literature in 1994.

Maeve Friel

Maeve Friel grew up in Ireland but now lives in a secret hideout in Spain with her husband Paul and her cat Pushkin. She is a successful writer of children's books, from young adult fiction to picture books and short stories. She has two sort of grown-up children.

Carlo Gébler

Carlo Gébler was born in Dublin, brought up in London and now lives in Enniskillen. He is married with five children. His favourite writer is the Russian short-story writer Anton Chekhov. He is the author of novels for both adults and children, as well as a journalist and critic. He has also directed a number of documentaries for British television including 'Put to the Test', a study of children sitting the Eleven-Plus exam in Ballysillan, north Belfast. 'Put to the Test' won the 1999 Royal Television Society award for the best regional documentary. His day job is writer-in-residence, Her Majesty's Prison, Maghaberry, Co. Antrim.

Sam McBratney

Sam McBratney grew up in County Antrim, Northern Ireland and still lives and works there. Once a teacher, he has now been a writer for over thirty years. He has written books for children of all ages and his work is known all over the world. His international awards include the Abby (America), the Silveren Griffel (Holland) and the Bisto (Ireland). His picture book *Guess How Much I Love You* is one of the most successful books in the history of children's literature.

Sam and his wife live surrounded by their children and grandchildren, and their tortoise, Mabel – who is the size of a dinner plate.

David O'Doherty

Born in Dublin in 1975, David O'Doherty's early work was characterized by its mediocrity, although teachers pointed to some promise in punctuality (satisfactory) and spelling (in Irish). The year 2000 saw the publication of his first children's book, *Ronan Long Gets it Wrong*, and the staging of his one-man play *The Story of the Boy Who Saved Comedy* at the Edinburgh and Dublin Fringe Festivals. His favourite things include cycling, pitch and putt and Scrabble.

Larry O'Loughlin

Larry O'Loughlin is an author and poet. To date he has written thirteen children's books. Most of his work is for readers of ten and under but he has also written two books for young adults.

Larry is an advocate for the rights of child labourers and supports the work of Mukti Ashram (Freedom House), a school outside Delhi, India, which is an education centre for freed child slaves.

Mark O'Sullivan

Mark O'Sullivan wishes he was a musician or a painter. Then again, if he were either of these things, he'd want to be a writer. Well, that's Sully (his nickname in the old soccer days) for you. He has written six novels for young people, and lots of short stories and poetry for those strange aliens who call themselves adults. Mark is married with two daughters in college who are both much smarter than he is. He doesn't think this is fair but, well, that's Sully for you again.

Siobhán Parkinson

Siobhán Parkinson's most popular book is the Bisto Book of the Year winner *Sisters – No Way!*, a funky version of *Cinderella*. If the world was a sensible place, *Four Kids,*

Three Cats, Two Cows, One Witch (maybe) would have won an award for daftest title, but it had to be content with a Bisto Merit award and a White Raven. *The Moon King* also received a Bisto Merit award and was an IBBY Honour Book, which meant that Siobhán got an invitation to lunch in South America. (She didn't go, because they forgot to send a plane ticket.)

Gordon Snell

Gordon Snell is the author of many novels, plays and books of verse for young people. He lives in Dalkey, on the coast of Ireland near Dublin, and is married to the writer Maeve Binchy.

Marilyn Taylor

Born and educated in England, Marilyn Taylor has lived in Ireland, working as a school librarian, for many years. Her most recent book *Faraway Home* – a true story of the Second World War set in Vienna, Dublin and Northern Ireland – won the Bisto Irish Children's Book of the Year Award. She has also published three modern novels of teenage life.

Married with grown-up children, her husband supplied much of the background to *Rainy People* from his own memories of growing up in Dublin during 'The Emergency'.

Michael Tubridy

Michael Tubridy lives in Dublin with his wife, Mary, and three children – Matthew, Daniel and Áine.

About his story, *The Boathouse*, Michael says: 'It's partly true. Years ago a pal and I locked two teachers in a boathouse, then ran away. The teachers spotted my pal but not me and he didn't squeal. Thanks, Peter!'

Gerard Whelan

Gerard Whelan, the author of four novels, is one of Ireland's best-known writers for young people. He is a former winner of the Ellis Dillon Memorial Award and the Bisto Book of the Year Award, while three of his books have been shortlisted for the Reading Association of Ireland Award and one was chosen by the International Youth Library for its White Ravens series. He lives in Ireland with his Dutch wife, Maria Ziere, and their weird son Davy – though it's only fair to say that Davy finds his parents pretty weird too.

Walter Macken
Flight of the Doves

Desperate to escape their vicious uncle in London, orphans Finn and Derval Dove embark on a dangerous journey across England to Ireland. Lonely and scared, their only hope lies in reaching the Connemara cottage of their beloved grandmother.

But for some reason their uncle offers a reward for their return and suddenly Finn and Derval find themselves at the centre of a nationwide search. Dogged every step of the way by people they don't know, who can the children trust . . . and how far will their uncle go to stop them reaching safety?

A classic Irish children's book.

Walter Macken
Island of the Great Yellow Ox

Ten-year-old Conor is in great danger. He has stumbled across the Great Yellow Ox, a treasure that has been hidden for over two thousand years. But two people, Lady Agnes and her husband the Captain, want it for themselves and will stop at nothing to get it.

When Conor and his friends are trapped on an island, only Lady Agnes and the Captain know where they are. As helicopters fly overhead and boats search the bay for the missing children, the boys find themselves in a desperate struggle, torn between wanting to escape and wanting to save the Great Yellow Ox.